# THE SA🜄URNIAN TALES

Chris Rabane, Ph.D.

Editions
Pandorama

First published in 2017

Editions Pandorama
Liège 4000, Belgium

ISBN: 2960194306
ISBN-13: 978-2960194302

To those who taught me English

# CONTENTS

# PREFACE

*The Saturnian Tales* is a collection of three stories about life, love and death intertwined with each other on an esoteric level.

*The Secret of the Saturn Room* tells the story of Stanislas Kromanov, a Russian count who lives in a magnificent manor with his servant Vera. Stanislas is a very predictable man, a creature of routines. His boring life changed forever when he met Yulia, a curious girl who turned his life upside down.

*FAPS-ROOM* is the story of a young, rich hedonist named Alan Donovan who created a secret society restricted to people under the age of 28. Alan is handsome, intelligent and carefree. He is also a drug addict who invented a very particular way to deal with his drug problems.

*The Diabolic Recipe for True Love* is about a young couple who almost died in a terrible car crash at the age of 18. A witness to the accident saved the couple with an ulterior, dark motive.

*The Saturnian Tales* should be read sequentially, starting with *The Secret of the Saturn Room*. If the tales are not read in the right order, they can spoil each other or be misunderstood.

CHRIS RABANE

# THE SATURNIAN TALES

# The Secret of the
# Saturn Room

Stanislas Kromanov was a wealthy Russian aristocrat who lived in his father's manor. He was a respectable count and the last surviving descendant of the Kromanovs. His father had mysteriously disappeared a year before the events narrated in this story took place. Stanislas inherited his father's manor, because the authorities had declared him legally dead. The magnificent house was located far west in the Russian Empire near the Barents Sea. It was a two-story building with sixteen rooms. Stanislas lived on the first floor with his servant Vera who took care of the entire manor. On the second floor, there were eight vacant rooms of identical size and shape. The door of each of these rooms was engraved with a symbol representing one of the different planets of the solar system.

Stanislas was a successful entrepreneur who worked most of the time. He had inherited the family business and owned two smelting factories that kept him extremely busy. In his late thirties, he married a 24-year-old girl from his town named Yulia. She was quiet, sensitive and very beautiful. Shortly after the wedding, Stanislas showed the rooms located on second floor of his manor to his wife. While the couple slowly walked from one room to the other, Stanislas proudly explained the history of the Kromanov family by commenting on the paintings of his ancestors. The couple visited each room except the one marked with a scythe, which is the symbol of Saturn. Without explaining why, Stanislas asked Yulia not to go into that room. She promised that she would never set foot in it.

# ♄

**SYMBOL OF SATURN**

Stanislas often left his manor to take care of his smelting factories. The first time he left Yulia alone, she kept her promise and did not visit the Saturn room despite wanting to know what was hidden there. The second time, her curiosity made her imagine horrible things that could explain why Stanislas did not want her to enter the Saturn room. She went to the second floor of the manor and walked nervously across the hallway from one room to the other. Yulia stopped walking when she arrived in front of the Saturn room. She stayed there for several minutes, staring at the scythe inscribed on the door. Her imagination was running wild. She knew that Stanislas was the only member of the Kromanovs who was still alive. She was imagining that he could have murdered family members to become the only heir to the Kromanov's fortune. She believed that corpses could be hidden inside the Saturn room. Unable to contain her curiosity, she rotated the doorknob to the room, realizing, to her surprise, that it was unlocked. She entered the room very briefly and noticed that it was a large chamber with many closets that looked like all the other chambers of the manor. Like in the other rooms, there was a painting of a member of the Kromanov family. It represented the great grandfather of Stanislas. Yulia felt relieved not to have found corpses. Nevertheless, her curiosity was not satisfied, because she did not know why Stanislas did not want her to enter the Saturn room. Late in the evening, Stanislas came home exhausted. He kissed her goodnight and went to bed.

When Stanislas left home again, Yulia decided to search all the closets of the Saturn room. In each closet, she found lots of documents and letters. Relieved, she left the room. Her husband came home very late. Before going to bed, he stared into Yulia's eyes for a couple of seconds.

"You really look tired," said Stanislas.

Then he kissed his wife and fell asleep. Yulia looked at herself in the mirror and realized that she looked exhausted. She was very upset because she still did not know why Stanislas asked her not to go into the Saturn room.

The next time Stanislas left his manor to run his business, Yulia was determined to check each document of each closet in the Saturn room. These documents were mostly related to the work of Stanislas's father. Yulia knew that her husband would be home at 8 PM sharp. She only had the time to read a couple of documents of the first closet. However, there were a dozen other closets that all contained files, binders and letters. She decided to stop her search and was relieved not to have found compromising information. At eight o'clock, Stanislas came home exhausted. He looked deep into Yulia's eyes and she felt guilty and uncomfortable.

"Did you enter the room marked with the scythe?" Stanislas asked.

Yulia tried to remain calm.

"Of course not," she said. "Why would you think something like that? I would never break a promise."

"You can tell the truth. I won't be angry." her husband said.

"I swear!" Yulia said. "I have never set foot in that room. I love you and will never lie to you!"

Stanislas looked at Yulia's face and thought that she had aged a lot since they were married. He kissed her goodnight and fell asleep.

The next morning, Yulia woke up and noticed little wrinkles on her face. She blamed them on the stress caused by the Saturn room and the lies she told to her husband. She knew that Stanislas had to leave town for an entire week for a business trip to Saint Petersburg. It was the ideal occasion to discover why she was not allowed to enter the Saturn room. Knowing what Stanislas could hide had become a real obsession for Yulia. Therefore, she planned to read all the documents she could find until she uncovered the truth. Monday, she spent the entire day in the forbidden room but did not find any relevant information. She hoped to find letters Stanislas had written to other women. At the end of the day, she was so tired that she fell asleep in the room. Tuesday, she continued her investigation and was so obsessed by finding compromising information that she forgot to eat. In the evening, she fell asleep in the Saturn room again. Wednesday morning, she noticed that her arms were terribly wrinkled. She immediately left the Saturn room to look at herself in the mirror, something she had not done since Monday morning. Horrified, she realized that she had aged enormously and looked like a 70-year-old woman. Yulia finally understood that she was not allowed in the Saturn room, because something was wrong with

the passage of time in this place that had deteri-
orated her youth.

Sunday night, Stanislas came home and did
not recognize the old woman who opened the
door. Yulia started to cry and told Stanislas that
she was his wife. She confessed that she had entered the Saturn room to explain her premature
aging. Stanislas said that his father never explained why he could not go into this room and
he had never questioned what his father said. He
just trusted him and never set foot in the room.

"That's why my father forbade me to go into
the Saturn room," said Stanislas sadly. "It was to
protect me. If he had explained why, I would
never have believed him. But where did you find
the key?"

When Yulia told Stanislas that the door was
not locked, he was terrified. He finally understood how his father could have disappeared.
Yulia died a couple of years later of bowel cancer
and Stanislas married another girl from his town
named Anushka. Before the wedding, Stanislas
locked the door of the Saturn room.

Anushka was a happy rebellious girl who
came from a very poor family. Stanislas fell for
her because she was remarkably smart. After the
wedding, Stanislas showed her the second floor
of his beautiful manor. He explicitly forbade his
wife to enter the chamber that was marked with
the symbol of Saturn. He explained that she
could not go there for her own safety because

"time passes more rapidly in the Saturn room" (to use his exact words). Anushka laughed and made fun of the weird safety recommendation of her husband. She agreed to never enter the Saturn room although she made it clear that she did not believe that time could accelerate in that location. Stanislas became suddenly angry.

"I try to protect you and you disrespect me," Stanislas said. "If you lay one foot in the Saturn room, I will divorce you at once!"

"Don't worry Stan, I won't go into this room," said Anushka trying to reassure her husband.

The first time Stanislas left home to take care of his business, Anushka did not enter the Saturn room. She thought that her husband was ridiculous to believe that a room could be cursed. Anushka asked herself, "How can a man as educated and intelligent as Stanislas believe such weird occult stuff? He must be hiding the real reason why I can't go into this room." Anushka started to spy on her husband. She wanted to know what Stanislas was doing in the Saturn room but realized that he never went there. The second time her husband left home, Anushka wanted to open the door of the Saturn room very briefly to uncover what it could hide. However, she realized that the door was locked. She looked for the key everywhere in the manor for two entire days but did not find it. Anushka concluded that Stanislas was so paranoid that he always carried the key with him. She was right and found the key in his pants when he had taken them off before going to sleep. Right after finding the key, Anushka quickly went to the Saturn room, unlocked the door and put the key back into Stanislas's pants. Anushka believed that she had outsmarted her husband. He would not know that the door of the Saturn room was open, because he never went there. Stanislas was a very predictable man. Every day, he did exactly the same things in the same order at the same time. If for some reason he broke his routines and went in the Saturn room, Anushka planned to blame their servant Vera to explain why the door was unlocked. Vera was a clumsy, old woman who was absentminded all the time. She was the perfect culprit. Anushka believed that she would soon discover the real reason why she could not go into the Saturn room. She just had to wait for her husband to leave the manor for his work.

The next time her husband left the manor, Anushka opened the door of the Saturn room very briefly. She noticed that it was a large room full of closets with a painting similar to the other rooms of the manor. She felt relieved not to have found anything alarming. Nevertheless, her curiosity grew stronger because she could not believe that her husband forbade her to enter the Saturn room because the passage of time was altered in that location. Late that evening, Stanislas came home and was very tired as usual. He kissed Anushka and they both went to sleep.

When Stanislas left home again, Anushka decided to make a little experiment to prove to her husband that the Saturn room was not cursed. Stanislas and Anushka had recently celebrated the first birthday of Vladimir, their big black cat. Anushka decided to leave Vladimir in the forbidden room during an entire day. She was absolutely sure that nothing bad could happen. She just wanted to show to her husband that Vladimir would still look young after staying a day in the Saturn room. Anushka believed that Stanislas would not care that she had used his key after realizing that the forbidden room was actually harmless. She put Vladimir in the room with a bowl of milk and some food. She did not enter the room herself, because she did not want to disobey her husband. The next day, she opened the door of the forbidden room to pick up Vladimir. The milk and the food were gone. To her great surprise, she did not see Vladimir. She called his name several times. Vladimir did not come. She entered the room to check whether Vladimir was not hidden under a closet. She looked under every closet. Vladimir was nowhere to be seen. She checked each closet one after the other but did not find him. Now, Anushka was really scared because Stanislas loved his cat. She finally left the room to check whether Vladimir was somewhere else in the manor. She looked for him everywhere in vain. Stanislas was home and said to Anushka, "You look awful today. What happened? Did you start smoking again?" Anushka was a heavy smoker before she was married but she had quit smoking after the wedding.

"What are you talking about?" replied Anushka and she went to the bathroom. She looked at herself in the mirror and realized that she did look awful. Anushka was a very rational girl and said to herself, "I am very anxious because Vladimir is missing. The stress and guilt make me look terrible today." She repeated these sentences twice in her mind to reassure herself.

"By the way, have you seen Vladimir lately?" asked Stanislas. "I haven't."

"Don't worry Stan, I just saw him playing in the garden a couple of minutes ago!" said Anushka, lying.

Anushka decided to go back in the Saturn room because Vladimir had to be there. There was no other rational explanation. She remembered that there were a lot of documents in the closets. Vladimir must have been hidden behind the documents when she searched the closets. Stanislas left town on a business trip in Saint Petersburg for an entire week. It was the ideal occasion to find Vladimir. Immediately after Stanislas left home, Anushka searched each closet thoroughly but did not find Vladimir. The closets were very high, almost two meters. One of the closets was near the window. Vladimir could have climbed on the curtains of the window and could then have jumped on top of this closet. Anushka needed a ladder because she was too short to check whether Vladimir was on top of the closet. She found one in the basement. When she arrived at the top of the ladder, she was able to see that there was a little skeleton on the closet. The skeleton was obviously Vladimir's. Anushka recognized his collar and her hands started to tremble. She suddenly realized that her experiment proved that Stanislas was right: time was passing so quickly in the Saturn room that Vladimir's body was already decayed. Anushka panicked and fell off the ladder. Her head hit the floor and she lay there unconscious for hours. Unfortunately, Anushka had kept the door of the Saturn room closed while she was looking for Vladimir. Her servant Vera had thus no idea of what had happened to her. She realized that Anushka was missing two days after her accident and did not find her, because she was forbidden to enter the Saturn room where Anushka was dying. When Stanislas came home after his business trip, he looked everywhere for Anushka, including in the Saturn room. Through the open door, he saw a skeleton lying on the floor near the ladder. Stanislas recognized Anushka's clothes.

After Anushka's death, Stanislas married Claudia who was the dumbest girl in town. He chose to marry her for that very reason. Shortly after the wedding, Stanislas showed her the second floor of his manor. They visited each room except the one marked with the symbol of Saturn. Stanislas explained that this room was a library where she could go every time she wanted to read.

"Reading once in a while won't kill you," Stanislas said, teasing his wife.

"Boooring!" Claudia said with an annoyed look on her face. "You know I hate books! Can't we just have sex now?"

Exactly nine months later, Stanislas and Claudia had a little girl and they all lived happily ever after. They named their daughter Tatyana. Fortunately, Tatyana hated books as much as her mother did.

# FAPS-ROOM

## **Warning**

*FAPS-ROOM* is a modern philosophical fable created in response to *Candide*, a French satire written by Voltaire and first published in 1759. The story of FAPS-ROOM was imagined in a world where most jobs are taken over by robots and aging is defined as a disease.

The reader should not imitate or believe Alan Henry Donovan, the hero of this story. *FAPS-ROOM* should be read entirely to be fully understood or it could lead to dangerous misinterpretations.

# CHAPTER 1
## HOW ALAN DONOVAN
## WAS RAISED

Alan Henry Donovan was only two years old in 1989 when his mother died of a heart attack. Her premature death played an important role in the development of Alan's unusual personality. He was raised by his father, the cold and distant Dr. James Donovan. James was a successful scientist who came from a wealthy family of doctors. He was the CEO of an American biotech company specialized in medical robots that made him a billionaire. Money had never been a problem for Alan. He inherited James's intelligence and good looks. However, unlike his father, he was not interested in medical sciences or in technology. He had been passionate about philosophy since he was only seven years old. One night, Alan asked his father to read him a bedtime story. James was a very rational and serious person who felt uncomfortable when telling stories to children. Instead of reading Alan a fairy tale, James preferred to tell him the story of a real person. He chose to talk about Diogenes of Sinope, an eccentric Greek philosopher, because he assumed that

Diogenes's adventurous life would entertain a seven-year-old. James explained Diogenes's story to Alan in the simplest way he could think of:

JAMES — Diogenes was happy, even though he was very poor. He was completely free and did what he wanted when he wanted. He chose to beg in the streets of Athens and slept in a huge ceramic jar.

ALAN — So he didn't have a job?

JAMES — Actually, he had a job, he was a philosopher, a great philosopher.

ALAN — And what does a philosopher do?

JAMES — He thinks about the human condition.

ALAN — But what does he do… I mean with his hands?

JAMES — He doesn't do anything. He thinks. Sometimes, he writes, sometimes, he teaches but he doesn't have to.

ALAN — This is so cool! And what did Diogenes write?

JAMES — We actually don't know… For him, philosophy was more a way of living.

ALAN — Awesome! I wanna be a philosopher!

JAMES — We'll see. [said James laughing] Someday you will become a doctor of philosophy.

James said this last sentence ironically thinking that his son would follow in his footsteps and become a successful scientist with a

Ph.D. just like him. He could not have been more wrong. Alan asked more questions:

ALAN — - Do you need to study if you wanna be a philosopher?

JAMES — - Not necessarily... Anyone who lives according to his personal beliefs can be considered a philosopher.

ALAN — - Can I be a philosopher from now on?

JAMES — - Yes, technically, but what are your personal beliefs?

ALAN — - I believe it's good to do what I want, when I want. From now on, I am a philosopher just like Diogenes!

JAMES — - Good for you. Now you're a seven-year-old philosopher! [said James ironically]

James could not take his little son seriously. But Alan was dead serious like kids sometimes can be at that age. He truly considered himself a philosopher. Every night he asked for more stories about philosophy. James was a scientist totally unprepared to raise a little kid on his own. To please his son, he kept telling him the only stories he really knew: the lives of the great thinkers that mostly included famous scientists and philosophers. Every night James took Alan on his lap and told him the life of another great philosopher, a bit in the same way normal parents tell fairy tales to their kids before going to bed. James discussed the lives of all the great philosophers, methodically and chronologically, from the ancient Greeks to the modern thinkers.

James talked about the great philosophers typically taught at school because they are politically correct like Plato, Aristotle, Voltaire and Jean-Paul Sartre. However, James was exhaustive in his storytelling and also talked about the authors who are rarely taught at school but who have shaped our modern way of thinking like Niccolò Machiavelli, the Marquis de Sade and Aleister Crowley. Alan absorbed all that knowledge like a sponge because he had an exceptional memory. Like most successful scientists, James had a very logical mind and it influenced Alan a lot. From an early age, he was taught to analyze life logically and he quickly became an atheist thinker, like his dad. However, Alan and his dad had very different personalities that influenced their understanding of atheism. James was a quiet and serious intellectual and his atheism led him to believe that life is an eternal quest for finding the Truth through a lifestyle based on honesty and hard scientific work. In contrast, Alan was a very fun guy and his understanding of atheism led him to believe that hedonism is the only logical lifestyle. In other words, he believed that a life without God should logically consist in pursuing pleasure and avoiding suffering.

Every night Alan harassed his father for more stories. When he was twelve, James could not take it anymore. Telling new stories every night about the great thinkers was very time-consuming. James decided to stop the storytelling and instead gently advised his son to read the philosophy books from his library. There was enough knowledge in the library to satisfy Alan's insatiable curiosity. However, Alan hated reading and suddenly lost interest in philosophy for many years. When Alan was a teenager, he was completely obsessed with sex. He lost his virginity at the age of thirteen to a French woman who was twice his age. Her name was Louise and she had worked as a maid in James's house since Alan had been eight.

Louise immediately loved the young Alan like a little brother. He looked like an angel with his curly blond hair and blue eyes. Louise was very shy and professional. She had absolutely no sexual interest in Alan. However, she was mesmerized by his intelligence. Alan loved to quote the great philosophers. Because Louise was not very educated, she was extremely impressed by a kid who sounded so sophisticated. A playful relationship rapidly developed between them that was completely platonic at first. Alan loved it when people read him stories. He sat on Louise's lap and she read short stories to him. This innocent little routine went on until Alan was nine. Then he tried to touch Louise's breasts when sitting on her lap. Louise struggled to distance herself from Alan but he always tried to create more physical intimacy with her. When Alan turned thirteen, she could no longer resist his playful attempts to seduce her and she decided to initiate him into the joys of sex. Every time James left the house, they hid in the attic and had sex. Louise was a great teacher and by the time Alan was fourteen, he already had more sexual experience than most men in a lifetime. As Louise grew older, Alan quickly lost sexual interest in her but they remained great friends. Alan was more attracted to girls closer to his own age.

# CHAPTER 2
## HOW ALAN DISCOVERED
## WHAT FAPS-ROOM STANDS FOR

Among the numerous thinkers James talked him about, Alan had been particularly influenced by eccentric libertines like the Marquis de Sade and John Wilmot. He completely embraced the famous precept of Fyodor Dostoyevsky stating that "If there is no God, everything is permitted." Alan was not an immoral person; he simply viewed life as a big party like most teenagers of his age did. However, he went further than regular teenagers because he wanted to live like a true atheist, fully committed to his philosophical beliefs. At the age of eighteen, he did not care about the future. Like all other teenagers, he did not think about growing old. He already smoked heavily and engaged in binge drinking several times per week. Moreover, Alan frequently consumed heroin with his spoiled, rich friends during the weekends. When Alan was eighteen years old, he enrolled in college but he was not interested in studying. He went to college only to party and meet more girls.

During Alan's freshman year in college, James became ill and was diagnosed with brain cancer. He did not reveal his condition to anyone, because he wanted to continue his work on medical robots. James kept going to his lab every day. After several months, his cognitive abilities started to decline but he struggled to do his job in spite of his disease. At the end of a long working day, he was so tired and distracted that he ran a red light on his way home. A truck hit his car and he died a couple of minutes later. Alan loved his father. He was completely depressed and consumed more heroin and alcohol to deal with his father's death. Alan was the only heir to James's fortune and estates. James possessed a huge country house out of town. It was located in the middle of a forest. James often went there with his wife Barbara during summertime. However, he stopped going to his country house after Barbara's death. He became a workaholic and focused all his energy on the development of his medical robots.

After James's death, Alan became the sole owner of the country house. Alan had only been in this house before Barbara's death, when he was a baby. He had therefore no memories about this place. After his father's funeral, Alan visited the entire country house and went to the basement to find wine in the cellar. To his great surprise, the door of the cellar was locked. He looked for the key everywhere but did not find it. Alan wanted alcohol so badly that he forced the door open with a crowbar. He did not find wine in the cellar but a strange machine that his father had invented. The device was encased in a metallic room. On the door Alan could read "FAPS-ROOM." Then he learned that a FAPS-ROOM was a medical device developed by Dr. James Donovan and his colleagues to perform assisted suicide of the terminally ill. FAPS-ROOM stands for Fully Automated Painless Suicide Room and was a top secret project. James installed a FAPS-ROOM in his country house, because he intended to die in dignity when his brain cancer would become worse and prevent him from having a normal life. He lived in a state where medically assisted suicide was forbidden, as in most US states.

Alan was very intrigued by the FAPS-ROOM. He read on the door that it was a fully automated device designed to minimize as much as possible all the horrors related to death. When engineering the FAPS-ROOM, James had been inspired by the philosophy of Epicurus about death. The Greek philosopher said, "Death does not concern us, because as long as we exist, death is not here. And when it does come, we no longer exist." James thought that humans make their lives miserable by dealing with death, because they do not understand that they actually do not have to and have forgotten Epicurus's wisdom. James said to himself, "If death does not concern us, we should let a robot handle this unpleasant matter." Then he started a scientific project to create that robot.

James was in expert in thanatology, which is the scientific study of death. As a young medical student, he had always been frustrated by the fact that most people considered death to be an inevitable source of pain not worth studying scientifically. Few physicians tried to develop reliable techniques to render the experience of death painless. In contrast, more efforts were made to decrease pain experienced during childbirth. James thought that rational human beings should focus as much attention on reducing the pain they experience when they leave this world as when they enter into it. Therefore, he became interested in the works of two great French physicians who were pioneers in his field of expertise: Dr. Joseph-Ignace Guillotin and Dr. Antoine Louis. At the end of the eighteenth century, Dr. Guillotin wanted to develop a method of execution that was more humane than the barbaric methods used at that time to kill people. Then his colleague Dr. Louis invented the guillotine, which is a very efficient apparatus to carry out death penalties by beheading. However, the guillotine was considered gruesome by many people because this technique involved the sight of blood and a decapitated head. Furthermore, there is evidence showing that some heads remained conscious for several seconds after the decapitation. Therefore, James wanted to invent a medical device that could produce a quick death painlessly in complete privacy.

After a complete review of the literature, James gathered evidence showing that the firing squad was the most effective and quickest way to execute inmates. By contrast, a typical lethal injection could take nine minutes to kill a person. Moreover, lethal injections often did not work as planned and death could occur even later. After reviewing the scientific literature, James found that shooting through the head was the method of execution that caused least pain. It was also the only method of execution that induced death almost instantly. James concluded that the fastest and least painful way to die was being shot in the head. He also believed that the best way for an inmate to die was being shot by a firing squad when he did not anticipate it. So he would not have to deal with the expectation of death, which is very stressful. Ideally, the inmate should be shot by the firing squad when he is asleep and sedated. Based on this reasoning, James imagined a machine that would recreate artificially this kind of ideal death in order to help people who want to commit suicide.

James developed FAPS-ROOM, a robot that automatically triggered sixty-four 0.950-caliber guns to assist someone in dying voluntarily. The person who wanted to end his life activated a program that did the shooting for him. Several terminally ill patients had used the FAPS-ROOM before James's death. They had followed the step-by-step procedures of the FAPS-ROOM's program to die more peacefully. The program was activated once the door of the FAPS-ROOM was opened. Then a screen was turned on automatically and a robot started to speak. The voice of the robot was based on James's voice. The robot explained that the person had entered a room especially built to assist his suicide within 40 minutes. The robot asked whether the person really wanted to commit suicide. If he replied that he wanted to end his life, he was invited to sit in a comfortable reclining chair in the middle of the FAPS-ROOM. The robot advised him to take painkillers like oxycodone or heroin to make his death as painless as possible. Then it explained precisely different options and what would happen within the next 40 minutes. The person could either press a button that triggered the 64 guns exactly at the same time or he could continue to follow the FAPS-program. In the latter case, he was invited to relax, to take sleeping pills and/or the drugs he liked. If he chose to remain conscious, he could do what he liked most: he could drink alcohol, watch the TV program he liked or listen to music. He could also chat with the FAPS-ROOM computer if he just wanted to speak since it was designed to entertain people. After 20 minutes, the medical robot was programmed to fire the 64 guns exactly at the same time over a time interval of 20 minutes. Thus, the subject did not know precisely when he would die, he only knew that it would happen.

At the moment of the shooting, artificial intelligence aimed 56 guns at the central nervous system of the subject and eight guns at his heart and all the guns were fired simultaneously. After the shooting, the room was automatically cleaned. The robotic device destroyed the remains of the reclining chair, dragged the corpse through a back door into a furnace that was part of the FAPS-ROOM. The corpse was cremated and the ashes were expelled from the FAPS-ROOM. A 3D printer was activated automatically and constructed a new reclining chair. Within 40 minutes, the FAPS-ROOM was completely clean and operational for the next kill. Because the FAPS-ROOM was controlled by artificial intelligence, it could handle two persons simultaneously in case a couple of terminally ill patients wanted to die together. However, fewer guns were used per person if two people were in the room. If the FAPS-ROOM computer detected more than two persons, the lethal program stopped.

The FAPS-ROOM was designed to avoid all the horrors related to death as much as possible. The machine was encased in a special sound-attenuating room that reduced the noise caused by the gunshots. The FAPS-ROOM killed a person faster than the traditional firing squad because there were more guns and each gun reached the brain and the heart at different angles with no overlap of the shootings. Thus, virtually all brain regions were destroyed at the same time making the central nervous system unable to process pain signals. The person was unconscious and dead within one second after the shooting. The lethality of the FAPS-ROOM was 100% based on the fact that all suicide attempts using this device had resulted in successful suicides. The FAPS-ROOM was thus more efficient than all the other traditional methods of suicide like suicide by firearms, drug overdose, drowning or hanging. From a legal point of view, the FAPS-ROOM could also be defined as a form of euthanasia where only the suicidal person and Dr. James Donovan (although dead) were morally involved. The FAPS-ROOM differed thus fundamentally from a firing squad, which is an effective execution method but involves the moral responsibility of several people.

James had initially created the FAPS-ROOM project for the terminally ill. Nevertheless, he wanted to extend its use to execute inmates. James was against capital punishment but wanted to provide a more humane way to kill people in US states where criminals are executed.

Alan injected himself with a large dose of heroin and lit a cigarette. Then he entered the FAPS-ROOM. He heard his father's voice giving him clear instructions on how to die. At the very end of his life, Alan heard the same reassuring voice that taught him so many things in his childhood. Dying seemed so easy that it was extremely tempting. A week earlier, Alan had started dating a cute girl named Alice but had not had sex with her yet. He said to himself that he would commit assisted suicide after having sex with Alice. The same day Alan had sex with her. It turned out that sex was so great that he put off his suicide. He even started to like Alice.

Alan and Alice had sex every night and Alan put off his suicide plan day after day. He could not help thinking about Alice's body all the time. After a couple of weeks, Alan was not depressed anymore and was able to think straight again. He realized that the FAPS-ROOM was giving him a new outlook on life and that he could end his life on a whim. Suddenly death was no longer tragic: the FAPS-ROOM allowed him to disappear off the face of the earth with no questions asked. As a devoted hedonist, Alan always thought that life should be a great party. With the FAPS-ROOM, life was a party again and Alan wanted to use the device to perfect his hedonistic lifestyle. In the meantime, he used heroin more frequently and became addicted to it. He also drank alcohol on a regular basis.

# CHAPTER 3
## HOW ALAN SOLD HIS FREE WILL TO A COMPUTER SCIENTIST NAMED TERRY BRADFIELD

A couple of weeks later, Alan was still hanging out with Alice. He liked her because she was smart and enjoyed talking about philosophy. However, they rarely agreed with each other and argued most of the time. One night, they met in a bar and Alan exposed his hedonistic views of life to Alice. He tried to explain why his binge drinking and womanizing behaviors made logical sense in a godless, absurd world. Alice believed that she could prove to Alan that life had a meaning and that he would pay the price for his selfish behaviors someday. Alan said:

ALAN     - If there is no God and no afterlife, isn't hedonism the only logical lifestyle?

ALICE     - I think your hedonistic lifestyle is irresponsible, pathetic and selfish.

ALAN     - Yes, but is it logical?

ALICE     - Maybe, but you need to fulfill obligations and be responsible to live morally with others.

ALAN     - Boooring!

Alan yawned on purpose and faked to fall asleep to mock Alice.

ALICE - How many times have you cheated on me since we have been together? Isn't that a convincing argument against your hedonistic lifestyle? I have suffered a lot since I met you.

ALAN - I never technically cheated on you. I said that I was a libertine and that we were in an open relationship.

ALICE - You said that after three weeks, when I wanted to clarify the status of our relationship. If I had known our relationship was going nowhere, I would never have slept with you.

ALAN - Who says that our relationship is going nowhere? We can have a serious, committed relationship later.

ALICE - Anyway, I just think that hedonism based on drugs is pathetic once you get older. How do you see yourself in your thirties?

ALAN - No thirties for me.

ALICE - What?

ALAN - You heard me well. I skip school, I skip the boring married life, I don't wake up before noon, I skip all the obligations of life and I skip being 30.

ALICE - Everyone is eventually 30, you can't just "skip" being 30.

ALAN    - Oh yes I can! I am an adventurer. I like danger. People like me never reach 30!

ALICE   - You can't be sure that you will die before you're 30 even if you're completely reckless. I am telling you: hedonism based on decadence makes no sense in the long run and is incompatible with true happiness.

ALAN    - Define true happiness. [said Alan ironically]

ALICE   - I can't give you a complete definition. But I think that a truly happy life is based on moral values like love, friendship, family, freedom... How can you be free if you're always under the influence of a drug?

ALAN    - Do you really think that you're free because you don't take drugs? Modern science questions the existence of free will. Your free will is nothing but an illusion, whether you're a junkie or not.

ALICE   - Don't you believe in free will?!

ALAN    - Come on, don't be naive. Your life choices result from complex genetic and environmental determinisms.

ALICE   - Maybe our behavior is under the influence of genetic and environmental determinisms. But we can still choose between good and evil. Science is not incompatible with God and free will.

ALAN    - Yeah, I know: Einstein was not an atheist, blah, blah, blah… It's always Einstein
when you no longer know what to say.
Grow up Alice, we're in the twenty-first
century and Einstein is dead! There is so
much evidence these days showing that
free will is just an illusion.

When Alan and Alice were arguing, they
were sitting on stools at the bar. The guy on Alice's side pretended to check his cell phone but
was actually listening carefully to the whole conversation. His name was Terry Bradfield and he
would later play a significant role in Alan's life.
Terry started to speak to Alan:

TERRY   - Hi, excuse me. I couldn't help overhear-
ing your conversation. I want to make a
deal with you.

ALAN    - Who are you?

TERRY   - I am Terry Bradfield. I am a computer
scientist who works on artificial intelligence in California.

ALAN    - Let me guess, you're one of these geni-
uses from the Silicon Valley who controls
the Internet? [said Alan laughing]

TERRY   - In some way… [said Terry smiling]

ALAN    - I am not interested in computer science.

TERRY   - You might be interested in what I do. I
work on intelligent humanoid robots. I
try to develop the algorithm of free will

to improve emotional intelligence in my robots.

ALAN     - Really? This is insane. Many scientists believe that free will does not exist.

TERRY    - Yes, you said that earlier to your girlfriend. You can help me with my project.

ALAN     - How?

TERRY    - I need someone's free will to develop an algorithm that will grant my robots the ability to distinguish good from evil. I understand that you don't believe in free will, right?

ALAN     - Yes, that's right.

TERRY    - Would you sell your free will for one thousand dollars?

Alan started to laugh and replied:

ALAN     - This whole conversation is absurd. How can I sell something that doesn't exist?

TERRY    - It's simple: you sign a form and I give you one thousand dollars.

ALAN     - Ok, where do I sign?

ALICE    - Don't do that.

ALAN     - I didn't know you were so superstitious.

ALICE    - You're a moron.

Alan signed a form stating "I hereby offer my free will to Terry Bradfield." In exchange, he received one thousand dollars. Then Terry left the bar. Alan thought that Terry was a lunatic. He said to Alice:

ALAN    - Can you believe this guy? He just gave me one thousand dollars!

ALICE   - And you just sold your free will. You won't be able to tell the difference between good and evil! Now, I wonder whether you had a free will in the first place...

ALAN    - Are you really naive? First, free will probably doesn't exist. Second, even if free will does exist, you can't just sell it by signing a piece of paper. That's absurd!

ALICE   - He stole your fee will and will transfer it into a robot!

ALAN    - You can't be serious? You can't believe this? That's not possible. Terry is just a crazy guy.

ALICE   - What if free will exists and you just sold it? What would happen to you?

ALAN    - Nothing because nothing happened when I signed that damn paper, except that I made one thousand dollars.

ALICE   - We really have different views about life.

ALAN    - Yes, you believe in silly things and I am realistic.

Alan and Alice continued to fight about their philosophical beliefs for another hour. Alice could not stand Alan's outlook on life that always had to be logical and rational. Then they left the bar to go to Alan's place. Alice had second thoughts and wanted to leave Alan for good because his materialistic view of the world was too irritating. On the way back, a homeless person was begging for some money. Alice gave him three quarters. Alan gave him one thousand dollars without thinking. Alice could not believe what she saw. She said:

ALICE    - You're not an asshole after all! I knew you had a good heart deep down.

Alice kissed Alan, who was surprised by his good deed because he had not planned it. He even wanted to take 500 dollars back. But he was happy about what Alice just said. Then they went home and had sex several times in a row. Alice was in love again, thinking that Alan was a great guy who just likes to act as if he did not care. She said to herself, "Actually he cares but he's too proud to admit it." She fell asleep around 2 AM. Then Alan lit a last cigarette, drank a last beer and injected himself with a high dose of heroin. He quickly fell asleep and had a very strange dream about his own life. In the beginning, his life was great. He saw himself in his early twenties living a life full of adventures and parties. He traveled to many countries and had sex with numerous gorgeous women. Around his twenty-eighth birthday, Alan dreamt that Death pursued him. The skeleton of Death was running after him with a bloody scythe. However, Alan outran Death and escaped. From afar he heard the skeleton shouting, "*Memento mori!*" Then Alan continued to dream about his adult life. At the age of 28, he was already severely addicted to heroin, cigarettes and alcohol. From that age, he started to cough a lot and suffered from chronic constipation. He was already in very poor shape. In his early thirties, he became sexually impotent and looked ten years older. Drugs had already severely damaged his looks. It was only the beginning of his fall from grace. As he aged, his life became more and more pathetic and meaningless. In his dream, he saw himself going to rehab and then relapsing. After the age of 35, his life was a vicious cycle of periods of heavy drug use followed by periods spent in rehabilitation centers. He was diagnosed with lung cancer at the age of 73. He died alone in a hospital two years later. At 5 AM, Alan woke up sweating with his heart racing. His hedonic lifestyle had finished in a terrible nightmare.

# CHAPTER 4
## HOW TERRY TRICKED ALAN INTO CREATING A CLUB RESTRICTED TO YOUNG PEOPLE

After his weird dream, Alan opened a bottle of vodka and drank directly from it. He realized how lucky he was to possess a FAPS-ROOM that would allow him to avoid a miserable, long life. Alan turned his computer on to find out on Google what his weird dream meant. However, he did not know that his computer had been hacked by Terry Bradfield, the person he supposedly sold his free will to. From his own computer, Terry subtly changed Alan's Google search results to influence his thoughts. In Alan's dream, everything was going well until he was pursued by Death holding a scythe. He googled "scythe symbol" to understand the symbolic meaning of the scythe. The first result was an article entitled "Saturn and hedonism in the twenty-first century." It was written and posted by Terry Bradfield, although his name did not appear on the webpage. After reading the article, Alan understood that the scythe is the symbol of Saturn[1]. He also uncovered the symbolism of Saturn. He read that Saturn is associated with time, the cycles of life and old age. It takes about 29 years for Saturn to orbit the sun and this revolution corresponds to the first Saturn return. The first Saturn return is considered to be the time a person fully reaches adulthood and must face the responsibilities of adult life. Then Alan looked up *"Memento mori"*, the two words that the skeleton of Death was shouting. He understood that *"Memento mori"* is a Latin expression meaning "Remember that you have to die." Alan realized that his dream was a warning telling him that he was just a mortal. He understood that his life would deteriorate dramatically after his first Saturn return. Alan was already severely addicted to heroin and knew deep down that the only way to quit this drug would be to go to rehab. He said to himself, "Fuck Saturn return! I will never stop doing drugs! Why should I go to rehab if I have a FAPS-ROOM?" Alan had already made up his mind and wanted to be logical until the very end of his life. He would never go to rehab, because the suffering it involved was terrible and incompatible

---

[1] For the readers who have not read the first Saturnian Tale, the astronomical symbol of Saturn is represented in black on the book cover, between the star and the pyramid.

with his hedonistic philosophical beliefs. It made no logical sense to suffer in a rehabilitation center for Alan if he possessed a FAPS-ROOM that allowed him to avoid the horrors of heroin withdrawal.

Alan continued to read Terry's webpage. It presented radical views on atheism and hedonism, the very foundations of Alan's life. As most hedonists, he believed that he should live in such a way that he maximizes net pleasure (pleasure minus suffering). However, Alan had never thought that his net pleasure could dramatically decline after his twenty-eighth birthday like in his dream. Terry wanted to influence Alan to make his hedonistic belief system more radical by taking net pleasure into account over a particular lifespan. On his website, Terry explained that atheists often choose the hedonistic lifestyle for logical reasons. If there is no God and no afterlife, it is logical to maximize net pleasure because everything is permitted as suggested by Dostoyevsky. However, Terry argues against hedonism that seeking net pleasure only works during a certain period and typically causes suffering in the long run. To make his point, Terry analyzed on a graph (Figure 1) how net pleasure typically varies over time in regular people and decadent hedonists. Terry defined net pleasure as the total amount of pleasure minus the total amount of suffering accumulated over a lifetime at a certain moment of death. For example, Figure 1B represents net pleasure in a typical decadent hedonist who takes a lot of drugs. If he dies at the age of 27, his net pleasure is extremely high, meaning that he experienced much more pleasure than suffering during his entire life. However, if the same decadent hedonist dies at 42, his net pleasure is negative with more suffering than pleasure during his life. In other words, the hedonistic lifestyle makes logical sense for people like Jim Morrison who died young. In contrast, other decadent libertines led miserable lives after their twenties like John Wilmot, who died at 33. Terry thus concluded that the old hedonist makes a mistake in his hedonistic equation. At 42, the hedonist, whose purpose is to maximize pleasure and minimize suffering, ends up having experienced less net pleasure than the 42-year-old regular person represented on Figure 1A.

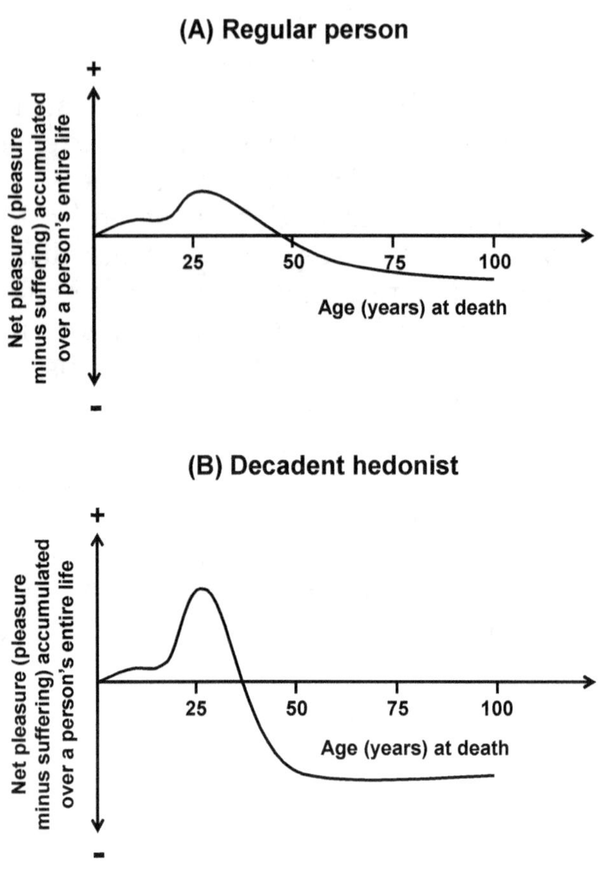


Figure 1. Net pleasure accumulated over a specific lifetime in function of the age at death in a regular person (A) and in decadent hedonist who experiences severe health issues after years of debauchery (B). Figure 1B illustrates the paradox of the hedonistic lifestyle: the hedonist is right to choose his lifestyle if he dies at 27 but wrong if he dies at 42. This figure was imagined by Terry Bradfield to manipulate Alan and is not based on scientific studies.

Terry ends his article with a very simple conclusion: atheist hedonists do not think their system through logically, because suicide is allowed in an absurd atheist world without afterlife. For them, death is simply the end of life. Since death must occur anyway, it does not really matter when, because atheist hedonists do not believe in an afterlife where they will be judged for their absurd, sinful life. Thus, in the perspective of atheist hedonism, death should occur right before the hedonist's health starts to deteriorate. From a purely logical point of view, death should occur immediately after the climax of the hedonist's life, because after this moment everything goes downhill and he is missing the purpose of his life: increasing net pleasure. Moreover, death should be induced voluntarily and painlessly, because natural death is usually painful and hedonists avoid pain. Finally, aging should be avoided because it is the longest way to die and causes suffering.

Terry concluded that hedonists should logically maximize net pleasure by taking lifespan into account and end their lives painlessly during a great party before their first Saturn return. At the end of the website, he wrote the following words:

*"Aging is the main cause of the existential problems of Homo sapiens. Unlike other animal species, Homo sapiens is aware of the aging*

*process and the slow decline of his intellectual and physical abilities. Aging is at the root of a universal neurosis because Homo sapiens has been tricked by an imaginary God into believing that aging is not a disease. However, he can never believe his own lie since he is the best witness of the gradual daily deterioration of his health. That neurosis makes him suffer more than all the other animals. The greatest paradox of the human condition is that the decadent atheist might be right or wrong to choose his lifestyle depending on how long he lives. Only the existence of an afterlife can prove him wrong if he dies young."*

Alan was thrilled by the radical ideas of Terry's website. He had finally found a philosophical system that analyzes hedonism completely and rationally from the beginning of the atheist's life until his death. Alan had always believed that the ultimate goal of evolved humans is to transform the daily boredom of life into a wonderful piece of art like a great movie with a beautiful ending. He wanted to dramatize the end of his life in a beautiful way. After reading Terry's website, Alan was convinced that he should end his life like a true hedonist: when net pleasure is highest during an awesome deathday party. The FAPS-ROOM of his country house was the perfect device for a painless death. Alan really liked the idea of finishing his life during a deathday party because it offered him the opportunity to not die alone but surrounded by his friends. He wanted to convince them to adopt his lifestyle and mindset in order to protect them from growing old miserably. Therefore, he decided to found a very selective club, organized like a secret society exclusively restricted to people under the age of 28. The symbol of Saturn would symbolize his society. The members of his club would help each other create a beautiful ending to their lives before they grow too old. Alan had many spoiled, rich friends who shared his materialistic outlook on life and were regular drug users. Some of them were already addicted to heroin. Others were severe binge drinkers on the verge of becoming full-blown alcoholics. Alan wanted to warn them against the dangers of drugs and convince them to end their lives painlessly in his FAPS-ROOM before their healths deteriorate. After careful analysis of his dream and Figure 1B, Alan decided that death would have a clear deadline in his secret society: the age of 27 years and 364 days. This definite deadline would discourage temptations to abandon the initial plan and postpone death.

At 7:30 AM, Alan went back to bed. Alice was sleeping like a log, unaware that Alan had been using his computer. She left the apartment at 8 AM and Alan slept until noon. He woke up with a hangover but was excited to create his new club. A week later, he broke up with Alice. He felt that she would never understand his philosophical theories about hedonism, life and death. He thought that they were morally incompatible.

# CHAPTER 5
## HOW ALAN CONVINCED
## HIS FRIENDS JACK AND JENNY
## TO JOIN HIS CLUB

From a very early age, Alan had considered himself a great thinker. He was therefore very proud to be the founder of the first club restricted to people under the age of 28. In reality, Terry Bradfield had imagined this secret society and had manipulated Alan from his computer. Moreover, other similar secret societies could have existed before. Alan considered his club to be his personal contribution to the hedonistic school of thought that originated in ancient Greece with Aristippus of Cyrene. Despite his intelligence, Alan naively believed that his secret society was the best way to protect his friends from the negative aspects of a debauched lifestyle. He honestly wanted to help his friends because they all smoked heavily and took drugs on a regular basis. However, they did not fully understand the risks of becoming drug addicts after using drugs frequently. They also underestimated the long-term effects of drugs on mental and physical health. First, Alan convinced his best friends Jack and Jenny to join his club.

Alan had known Jack since he was thirteen. Jack was one year older than Alan. He was dim-witted but very fun. At the age of 20, Jack was already a heavy binge drinker who often engaged in risk-taking behaviors like driving fast or fighting in bars. Alan invited Jack to his country house to smoke crack cocaine and drink beer. He asked Jack:

ALAN — Where do you see yourself in your thirties?

JACK — I don't know.

ALAN — Are you interested in a particular job?

JACK — Not really. What a weird question. Why should I work? My parents are rich. Are you drunk?

ALAN — No, I wanna know what you like. We never talk about that stuff. What are your interests in life?

Jack thought for a few seconds trying to give an answer:

JACK — Driving fast, sex and alcohol.

ALAN — And what else?

JACK — Seriously? Why do you care?

ALAN — I am your friend and wanna know what you like.

JACK — I like partying, music, porn, that kind of stuff...

ALAN — So, you like drinking, sex and driving.

JACK       - Yes, that's pretty much all I like... and heroin. I like doing heroin!

ALAN       - And how long will you live that way?

JACK       - What do you mean?

ALAN       - Do you see yourself drinking and doing heroin during your entire life?

JACK       - Yes, why not?

ALAN       - You're a moron.

JACK       - Why?

ALAN       - Have you seen drug addicts or alcoholics in their forties?

JACK       - You mean homeless people?

ALAN       - Not exactly.

JACK       - I can't become homeless, my father is rich.

ALAN       - Do you believe in God?

JACK       - Like believing that a tall, old guy with a long, white beard lives somewhere in the galaxy?

ALAN       - Yes, do you believe that a tall, old guy with a long, white beard created our planet?

JACK       - Maybe... Who else created our planet?

ALAN       - Anyway, do you go to church?

Jack started to laugh and replied:

JACK       - No.

ALAN       - What do you think is gonna happen once you die?

Jack did not know how to answer this question. Some seconds later he said:

JACK       - My parents will put my body in a grave.

ALAN    - And? Then?

JACK    - Then??? Nothing. I am in the grave.

ALAN    - You don't think your spirit will survive and go to heaven for example?

JACK    - No, I think my spirit will be trapped in the coffin. And I think my spirit will die and decay in my brain.

ALAN    - Thus, you don't believe in an afterlife.

JACK    - I never thought about it but not really. I don't care.

ALAN    - Jack, you can't live like a pig your entire life. Someday, your life will be pathetic. If you keep drinking and driving drunk, you will either become an alcoholic or die in a car accident.

JACK    - I hope I will die in a car accident!!

ALAN    - Really?

JACK    - Yeah, that's why I never wear my seat belt. I don't wanna survive a car accident and be a crippled!

ALAN    - That doesn't make any sense... And the airbags?

JACK    - There are no airbags in my car. I always drive my old Porsche 911, the one my father gave me for my sixteenth birthday.

ALAN    - That's why you're still driving that old Porsche... You're smarter than I thought...

JACK    - I know that I am not as smart as you. Actually you can call me stupid. But sometimes I have good ideas, like not wearing my seat belt.

ALAN   - But what if you don't die in a car accident?

JACK   - But I will die in a car accident. You know how fast I drive.

Suddenly, Alan felt outsmarted by his dim-witted friend. Jack drove very fast and was completely irresponsible all the time. The odds that he would die in a car accident were extremely high and he did not need the complex logistics of Alan's club to die young. Alan realized that he was trying to convince an idiot with logic. Then he said:

ALAN   - I am going to create an awesome club for people under the age of 28 with drugs, beer and sex!

JACK   - Terrific! I wanna be in your club!

ALAN   - Yes, but the club is restricted to people under the age of 28. That means that

JACK   - I am 20!

ALAN   - Let me finish. When members turn 28, they are either expelled from the club or they end their lives during a deathday party.

JACK   - I don't care, I will never be 28!

Alan then explained what a deathday party is. Jack kept saying that he would be dead before his twenty-eighth birthday.

Alan went to Jenny's place to convince her to join his club. She was one year younger. Jenny was a promiscuous, average-looking girl completely obsessed with her looks. Her big breasts were the only thing she liked about her body and she liked to show off her cleavage. She could not stand the idea of growing old and seeing her breasts sag. She liked Alan a lot and they had slept together many times. Alan said:

ALAN — - Jenny, do you wanna have kids some day?

JENNY — - Oh no, I don't wanna have kids!

ALAN — - Why not?

JENNY — - I don't wanna ruin my breasts. Have you seen them? They are so beautiful, big and firm. They're all I have.

ALAN — - I know that, they are awesome. But they will eventually sag.

JENNY — - I can't even think of that. They are so big that it can happen soon. If only scientists could discover a cure for aging and we could be young forever!

ALAN — - We will have to wait for that. I have a more practical way to solve the problem of aging. Do you believe in God?

JENNY — - No.

ALAN — - Do you believe in an afterlife?

JENNY — - I wish I could but I can't imagine an afterlife without God...

ALAN — - What is the purpose of your life?

JENNY — - I don't know... I like to hang out... I think my life is absurd. I have no talents. Does your life have a meaning?

ALAN     - Yeah: having fun and avoiding pain and the boredom of daily life.

JENNY    - That seems so logical. Why do you go to college?

ALAN     - To party and meet girls. I go to college to have fun.

JENNY    - You always have a logical answer for everything! So you want to party during your entire life? Isn't that boring? Someday you will be old and pathetic!

ALAN     - No, I won't. It isn't possible to remain young forever but it's possible to never grow old.

JENNY    - Yeah, if you're lucky enough to die young...

ALAN     - I will die young.

JENNY    - How can you be sure?

ALAN     - Shouldn't we decide when to end our lives?

JENNY    - Yes, I think we should be able to choose. But society will never let us end our lives when we want to.

ALAN     - Fuck society! I am totally free. I want to control my life and its ending!

JENNY    - Me too, but I don't have the guts to kill myself. I am sure I will fail my suicide. I screw up everything.

ALAN     - Imagine you could disappear from this absurd world by simply pressing a light switch.

JENNY   - That would be cool... I do it right now...
I don't wanna go to school tomorrow!

ALAN    - That's how I'm planning to die. I've created a club restricted to people under the age of 28. Members can end their lives painlessly, using a medical robot.

JENNY   - That's insane!

ALAN    - I don't wanna die the old-fashioned way.

JENNY   - Me neither, but we have to.

ALAN    - Why? You're an atheist.

JENNY   - I don't know why. Is the medical robot the modern way to die?

ALAN    - In some way, it's the modern version of hara-kiri. You die voluntarily with honor rather than miserably in a nursing home over several decades.

JENNY   - Hara-kiri is the ritual of the Samurai. They were proud warriors with an honor code.

ALAN    - Maybe, but you still have to clean their blood and guts after their suicide. I prefer the medical robot.

JENNY   - I don't know about the robot... But when I imagine my life after 30, I wish there was a way out.

ALAN    - My club is the easy way out.

JENNY   - It's the sleazy way out!

ALAN    - Sleazy or easy, it's a way out. What's your plan?

JENNY     - I am just like everyone else: I don't have
          a plan. I can barely plan my day. How
          could I plan my life and my death?
ALAN      - With the help of my club. If you become
          a member of my club, you won't have to
          worry about anything. You will never
          grow old. Your wonderful breasts will
          never sag.
JENNY     - It's very tempting... Not worrying about
          the future... Not worrying about my
          looks... Never growing old... living like a
          kid...
ALAN      - Think of it: you need to die anyway. You
          should see adult life as a long and boring
          to-do list and death is the last item on the
          list. However, there's a trick: you can
          erase the entire to-do list if you start with
          the last item.
JENNY     - If you put it this way, I don't want an
          adult life.
ALAN      - Why do we need an adult life? I don't
          want responsibilities. I don't want to
          wake up in the morning to go to work. I
          don't want to marry someone I will di-
          vorce three years later. I don't want to
          have kids who will live in an over-
          crowded, polluted hell!
JENNY     - Me neither, fuck adult life!

Alan and Jenny continued to talk about how
much adult life sucks. Alan then explained the
rules of his club to her. Jenny had a crush on Alan

and considered that being a member of his club was a good opportunity to spend more time with him. She wanted to join Alan's club but she had moral objections:

JENNY — Your club is tempting but it seems immoral. You really have a sick, twisted mind...

ALAN — A robot-assisted suicide is not immoral if we know that we are condemned to die slowly over several decades from age-related diseases.

JENNY — I don't understand, what do you mean?

ALAN — I mean that we can now narrow down all the causes of our deaths to some terrible diseases. Our modern world is so safe that most people will die of degenerative diseases or cancer after the age of 70. Do you want to die of cancer?

JENNY — No.

ALAN — Do you want to die of Alzheimer's disease?

JENNY — I don't know that disease.

ALAN — Alzheimer's is a dementia that kills you typically over a decade. Imagine that you slowly become a moron until you're not even capable of eating alone. You become so dumb that you forget to feed yourself. You forget to shower, you live in your filth like an animal.

JENNY — That's disgusting! I don't want that!

ALAN    - And what would you do if you knew you had cancer or Alzheimer's?

JENNY   - I would kill myself!

ALAN    - How?

JENNY   - I don't know… with a gun.

ALAN    - That's what a robot-assisted suicide is all about. It's more efficient than a gun.

JENNY   - Ok, I get it now. It's either a slow painful death or a quick painless robot-assisted suicide… The medical robot is the lesser of two evils.

ALAN    - Now you get it. And besides, let's face it: I am a spoiled, rich kid. I am a parasite. The sooner I die, the better. Almost all the members of my club will be parasites like me. We will commit altruistic suicides and stop polluting the world. The world will be better off without us.

JENNY   - It's the suicide idea that bothers me most. It seems wrong…

ALAN    - It's wrong if God exists.

JENNY   - But I think he doesn't exist… It's wrong for other reasons I can't explain…

ALAN    - The only problem I see is the existence of an afterlife where I have to pay the price for committing suicide.

JENNY   - But I don't believe in an afterlife.

ALAN    - In that case, why is my club immoral?

JENNY   - I don't know, it just seems immoral. The suicide idea bothers me.

ALAN    - To end your life in a FAPS-ROOM is not a real suicide. It can be considered a form of euthanasia performed by a doctor with the help of a robot.

JENNY   - Who's the doctor?

ALAN    - My father Dr. James Donovan.

JENNY   - But he's dead.

ALAN    - Maybe but he's morally responsible because he created the FAPS-ROOM.

JENNY   - That doesn't make any sense. Your father is dead.

ALAN    - From a certain point of view, you ask my father to perform euthanasia through the help of a robot.

JENNY   - Thus, no one is responsible because a dead person performs euthanasia?

ALAN    - I am not saying that. However, artificial intelligence creates a sort of ethical loophole in the practice of euthanasia.

JENNY   - Thus, a single person who is already dead becomes a scapegoat for many other deaths?

ALAN    - In some way but we could argue a lot about this interpretation.

JENNY   - It's pure cynicism!

ALAN    - If you don't want to join my club, that's OK. I respect your point of view.

JENNY   - I haven't actually said that. I don't want to grow old and I think you're club is wrong. Actually, I don't know what I want.

ALAN      - It's up to you.
JENNY     - I wanna join your club despite the fact
            that it's morally wrong. It's tempting be-
            cause it's easy.
ALAN      - That's good enough for me. It's your
            choice.

Jenny tried to find other arguments to discredit Alan's club. She finally agreed to be a member because she could leave the club whenever she wanted anyway.

Although Alan hated discipline, his club needed some ground rules to function properly. His very selective club was restricted to people under the age of 28. Thus, members had to be expelled from it right before their twenty-eighth birthday. Moreover, his club needed to remain hidden from society because it was breaking many US laws by using a FAPS-ROOM illegally to practice assisted suicides. To belong to the club, each member had to swear that he would respect three fundamental rules:

I. Each member must be under the age of 28. Membership has an expiration date and expires the last day a member is 27, just before he turns 28. Each member must tattoo the astronomical symbol of Saturn followed by his expiration date on his chest, at the level of his heart.

   • If a decadent life does not kill a member before his twenty-eighth birthday, he is invited to end his life on his expiration date by means as painless as possible using a FAPS-ROOM after a deathday party.

• If a member changes his mind and decides to grow older than 27, he is banned from the club for life and never allowed to contact the other members again.

II. No one (past or present member or anyone who wanted to join the club but changed his mind) can reveal the existence of the club under penalty of death.

III. Alan Henry Donovan is the founder and president of the club. After Alan Henry Donovan's death, the oldest member of the club becomes president.

Alan created the second rule in order to deter people from speaking about the club. It was absolutely essential that his club remained secret. Nevertheless, Alan knew that he would never murder a person for revealing the existence of the club. In practice, he would ridicule and discredit this person so that no one would believe him. However, no one but the president could know that the people who talk about the club would not be murdered. Alan decided to share this secret information with the next president, immediately before his own suicide. The new president then told this information to the next one, etc.

Alan wanted to limit the number of rules in his club. He realized that female members should not be pregnant for a lot of ethical and practical reasons. The children born in the club would all be orphans. However, he felt that forbidden pregnancy was incompatible with freedom and his members should remain as free as possible. Alan decided to simply discourage pregnancy by explaining how difficult it would be to take care of children who would eventually become orphans.

Alan's friends frequently asked him the name of his club. However, Alan decided not to name it. He believed that it would be easier to conceal his club from society if it had no name. Therefore, his secret society would simply be referred to as "the club."

Alan did not want to advocate suicide. He was actually more interested in a wild, carefree life that ends suddenly before the age of 30. This is why he loved his friend Jack so much. Jack was a rebel but he was too dumb to know what he was rebelling against. Jack reminded Alan that ignorance is bliss but one has to be blessed with stupidity to live by this precept. Alan knew deep down that he was cursed with the kind of high intelligence that makes the life of the great thinkers miserable. He believed that rational minds ruin the beauty of life by overanalyzing it. This is one of the reasons why he used alcohol and heroin: he wanted to shut down his rational mind. Alan believed that dying young keeps the beauty of life intact. In contrast, growing old gradually reveals all the flaws of a human being that were initially concealed by his youth. According to Alan, James Dean, Jim Morrison and Jimi Hendrix had lived the most perfect lives. He particularly loved Jim Morrison's music because he shared with him the same mystic fascination for life and death. Alan wanted to remain a wild child forever, just like Jim Morrison.

Alan thought that James Dean, Jim Morrison and Jimi Hendrix had lived short, intense lives because medical sciences and technology were not very advanced in the twentieth century. In other words, they could have survived their fatal accidents if they had lived in the twenty-first century. After 2000, cars became safer and many people always had their cell phone to call an ambulance immediately after an accident. Consequently, people who were involved in an accident or who overdosed were rushed to the hospital at the right time. Then they received better medical treatments than during the twentieth century. Thus, medical sciences and technology had made so much progress after 2000 that dying from a drug overdose, an accident or a disease before old age was very unlikely. Alan thought that the twenty-first century was not a good time for decadent hedonists, because they rarely died before their lives were totally ruined by drug addiction.

He considered that his club was an update of decadent hedonism that allowed this school of thought to survive in the twenty-first century in spite of all the scientific progress that had been made.

Alan used his country house to organize never-ending parties of debauchery. This place was ideal, because it was located in the middle of a forest and the noise caused by the parties could not disturb anyone. Alan's father loved nature and kept animals in his country house like ducks, pigs and deer. Therefore, the house was permanently occupied by a housekeeper who was in charge of the animals and the estate. After creating his club, Alan hired servants to clean the country house and keep it filled with luxurious food. He also hired two nurses, because accidents were frequent during his parties.

After recruiting Jack and Jenny, Alan persuaded other people among his friends to become members of his club. Most of them used drugs on a regular basis. Alan did not talk about his assisted suicide plan immediately but performed a rigorous selection process to determine who would deliberately commit to the rules of his club. Alan only wanted to recruit people who were fully aware of the philosophical foundations of his club that were based on his updated version of hedonism. Therefore, he wanted to know the religious beliefs and motivations of his future followers. He asked his friends if they believed in

God and if they were attracted to sex, drugs and alcohol. If they answered that they believed in God and/or were against drugs, Alan simply explained that his club was not for them, because their religious beliefs were incompatible with his. If people answered that they were atheists and liked drugs, Alan invited them individually to his house for an interview to further examine their philosophical beliefs. During the interview, Alan presented the basic ideas of his club on a PowerPoint presentation. First, he introduced the potential member to the concept of hedonism pioneered by Aristippus of Cyrene, which consists in maximizing net pleasure. Then he talked about the negative effects of drugs and alcohol on health that typically occur after many years. Finally, he showed the figure of Terry Bradfield's website depicting how net pleasure typically evolves over the lifetime of decadent drug addicts (Figure 1). After the PowerPoint presentation, he asked the potential member, "Would you prefer to die naturally from a disease or in an accident, or would you prefer to die voluntarily, instantly and painlessly?" Then Alan explained that dying instantly and painlessly is technically possible with the right technology. If the potential member asked how it was possible, Alan simply answered that the technology existed and was available in America but he never revealed that he possessed a FAPS-ROOM to a nonmember. If the potential member preferred to die naturally,

Alan explained that he could not belong to the club for philosophical reasons. If the potential member preferred to die painlessly and instantly, Alan explained that a true hedonist should include his own lifespan in the hedonistic equation. He explained that hedonists become the victims of their own philosophy if they keep living once their bodies are damaged after several years of drug use. Alan pointed at Figure 1B with his finger at the level of age 28 and, in the meantime, asked the following question, "Are you willing to die painlessly and instantly using the right technology just before your twenty-eighth birthday knowing that it would be impossible to die painlessly in the same way later?" Alan then explained that a painless and reliable suicide assisted by a robot has nothing to do with the traditional methods of suicide that are typically painful and often fail. He explained the numerous technical problems related to committing suicide by firearms, drugs, drowning, wrist cutting or hanging. If the potential member answered that he did not want to die before the age of 28, Alan explained that the club would not assist him to commit suicide later and that the club was thus not for him. If he answered that he was willing to die voluntarily and painlessly before the age of 28, Alan asked whether he would commit to the three rules of his club. If he accepted, he became a member and Alan explained how a FAPS-ROOM works.

After being accepted into the club, the new member had to go through initiation rituals. He had to inject himself with a large dose of heroin. Then the other members tattooed the symbol of Saturn on his chest followed by his expiration date. In the meantime, the new member had to swear that he would never reveal the existence of the club and that he would respect its rules. His new life started within the club and would last until his death. The new member was initiated into hedonism and libertinism. He also learned the art of contemplating his own death. He was taught to view death not as something to fear but as a motivating factor to live fully during his youth. In Alan's secret society, death represented the end of youth and was a convenient way to avoid the miseries of old age. Each new member was encouraged to reflect on a simple idea: since death is inevitable, it might as well occur painlessly at the right time in order to avoid suffering, diseases, aging, boredom, poverty and overpopulation.

When a member was about to turn 28, the club organized an amazing deathday party, especially tailored for him. The party took place the day before his twenty-eighth birthday. A deathday party was intended to facilitate the transition from life to death in the smoothest and most painless way possible. It was supposed to be the best party of a member's life. Alan wanted to replace the anguish of death by the anticipation of a great event. A deathday party involved a sequence of rituals aimed at preparing the nearly-28-year-old member to accept that his death was not tragic but should be viewed as a release from life's absurd duties. Every deathday party comprised luxurious food that included the favorite meal of the nearly-28-year-old member, mind-blowing sex and drugs taken during a suicide ceremony. During a deathday party, members were given access to all the food, sex and drugs they wanted. Deathday parties were therefore also called *ad libitum* parties: food *ad libitum*, sex *ad libitum* and drugs *ad libitum*. The party started early because the nearly-28-year-old member had to enter in the FAPS-ROOM 40 minutes before his expiration date, thus before midnight. However, the entire deathday party lasted until dawn and even later, because life must go on for the other members.

It was important to convince everyone that all the members of Alan's club were alive to conceal the existence of his secret society. Some days before the deathday party, the nearly-28-year-old member gave his cell phone and computer to the other members of the club. Then he explained with whom he interacted on a regular basis and how. He also communicated all his passwords and usernames to the other members to allow them to use his cell phone and emails. The club was thus able to answer the messages of the family and friends of the nearly-28-year-old member after his death. Since all the members of Alan's club came from dysfunctional families, they practically never spent time face-to-face. They usually communicated poorly through texting, Facebook and emails. For practical reasons, the members were asked to cancel their Facebook accounts, because updating a dead person's Facebook page to pretend that he was alive involved a lot of work. In contrast, answering emails and texting was easier and less time consuming.

Alan had imagined the perfect ruse: no one discovered that the members of his club had committed suicide before their twenty-eighth birthday, because there were no corpses. Moreover, the dead members were reported missing after a very long time. In most cases, the family of a dead member kept sending text messages and emails to the deceased member without realizing that the other members of the club answered all the messages on his behalf. The masquerade lasted for months and sometimes for years. The police had absolutely no idea that the missing persons they were looking for were all connected to Alan's deathday parties.

Alan wrote down the rules and the logistic aspects of his club in a pamphlet. The astronomical symbol of Saturn appeared on the first page. In his pamphlet, Alan added ideas about hedonism that he copy-pasted from Terry Bradfield's webpage. After finishing the manuscript, he felt completely relieved: he was nineteen years old and had eight years of total freedom ahead of him. His father's fortune was important enough to allow him to live an idle and luxurious life until his twenty-eighth birthday. Alan printed the pamphlet and distributed it to all the members of his club.

# CHAPTER 6
## HOW ALAN KEPT SMOKING
## WHERE HE WANTED

After founding his club, Alan went to a bar in his town with Jenny and Jack to binge drink. They ordered tequila bottles and started to do shots. Alan lit a cigarette. However, the law prohibiting smoking in public places had just taken effect in his city. Alan decided to ignore the law, because it was against his philosophical beliefs. For him, smoking in bars and restaurants was a matter of personal freedom. He advocated that everyone should fight for his or her rights. He tried to convince all smokers to follow his example. He believed that if everyone disobeyed the law prohibiting smoking, it would be abolished like the prohibition of alcohol in the 1930s. The waitress asked Alan to stop smoking. She was a tall redhead with freckles on her face. Her name was Wendy. Alan had just seen her smoking outside in the rain during her break. Wendy said:

WENDY  - Excuse me, you can't smoke in here.

ALAN    - Do you smoke? [asked Alan, knowing the answer]

WENDY  - Yes, but outside.

ALAN     - And how does your cigarette taste in the rain? [asked Alan smiling]

WENDY  - Terrible. [answered Wendy shyly]

ALAN     - Do you like to smoke in the rain? [said Alan smiling]

WENDY  - No.

ALAN     - So, why do you do something you don't like?

WENDY  - To be frank, I wouldn't have voted to ban smoking in bars. But the law is the law.

ALAN     - But a law can be abolished. We live in a democracy. At the end of the day, we make the law. Imagine now that most people rebel against a particular law. Imagine that we could persuade the majority to smoke inside again. We would be free again, like in the twentieth century.

Wendy smiled.

WENDY  - What's your name?

ALAN     - Alan.

WENDY  - My name is Wendy.

ALAN     - You don't smoke here because you don't wanna lose your job. I get that. I will tip you ten dollars for each cigarette. Let me talk to your boss about our deal and we will smoke in the back.

Alan and his friends went into the back of the bar and drank until they were completely wasted. Alan invited Wendy and the barman to drink tequila with them. He paid for all the bottles. Everyone was drunk and Alan put his hand around Wendy's waist. She was not particularly attractive. Alan said:

ALAN    - Why are you a waitress? You could be a model. You're tall and thin.

Wendy giggled and said:

WENDY - You just want to fuck me so you can come again and smoke in the bar with your buddies.

ALAN    - Yeah, you're right. I am too drunk to smooth-talk you. I will just leave.

WENDY - No, don't leave. I never said I didn't want to fuck.

And Wendy kissed Alan. They were French kissing right in front of Jenny who became extremely jealous. She slapped Alan in the face and said:

JENNY   - You disgust me, Alan!

ALAN    - What's wrong with you? Why do you care?

Jenny was drunk but not drunk enough to reveal her romantic interest to Alan out loud. She did not know how to respond and finally said:

JENNY   - How would you react if I kissed the barman?

ALAN    - What? I would laugh. Kiss him, go ahead.

The barman looked at Jenny timidly. He was a short, fat guy in his forties. He was drunk enough to muster the courage to grab Jenny's hand. Jenny screamed:

JENNY  - Get away from me!

BARMAN - But you just said…

JENNY  - I was just trying to make a point. We are not a bunch of monkeys!

ALAN   - Actually we are. Haven't you seen documentaries about bonobos? They are just like us.

WENDY  - Bonobos?

ALAN   - Small apes completely obsessed with sex, no strings attached.

WENDY  - Really?

ALAN   - There are no couples among bonobos. They form an ideal society of libertines. Everyone mates with everyone! And their society works better than ours!

JENNY  - Of course, you like bonobos!

ALAN   - The bonobo should be the mascot of our club!

WENDY  - What club?

JENNY  - Oh, shut up Alan! Don't pay attention to what he says. He's drunk, he doesn't know what he's talking about.

At 2 AM, it was closing time and everyone had to leave the bar. Alan, Jenny, Jack and Wendy decided to keep drinking in Jack's place because he lived only five blocks away. Jenny and Jack continued to drink and smoked pot until 4 AM. They were both sitting on the couch in the living room. Jack tried to kiss Jenny, who rejected him aggressively. Then he tried to grab her boob and she slapped him in the face. In the meantime, Alan had sex with Wendy in Jack's room. When Jenny heard Wendy reaching orgasm, she said to Jack:

JENNY   - Ok, I've changed my mind, let's do it!

But Jack was asleep. She said:

JENNY   - Wake up idiot! It's your lucky night.

Jack and Jenny had sex on the couch. The next morning, Alan convinced Wendy to join his club and she agreed. Alan had found a bar where he could smoke in peace with all his drinking buddies.

# CHAPTER 7
## HOW ALAN MET HIS CRIPPLED
## FRIEND DAVID

One year after its creation, Alan's club had attracted 20 members. Alan was very happy with this number, because it was easy to handle. He was relieved that the oldest member was 25 years old. He had two years ahead of him before the first deathday party.

David Darteuil was the oldest member of the club. He was French. Alan met him in La Tour d'Argent, a famous Parisian restaurant. Alan often went to France with his friends when smoking was still allowed in French restaurants and bars. One night, they partied until 10 AM. Alan and his friends returned to their hotel located in the fifth arrondissement. They woke up hung over at 7 PM and went to La Tour d'Argent to eat. Next to their table, a guy in a wheel chair was eating alone. He looked very depressed and had drunk several bottles of wine. This guy was David Darteuil. He was chain-smoking and stared blankly at his ashtray that was full of cigarettes butts. Alan asked:

ALAN     - Are you all right?

DAVID    - What do you think? [replied David aggressively with a French accent] I am in a fucking wheelchair, idiot!  I will never be able to fuck again!

ALAN     - Are you sure? I heard that some paraplegics could still get it up...

DAVID    - Not me, I was injured at the wrong level...

ALAN     - What happened?

DAVID    - I fell off the third floor... I was drunk...

And David explained his tragic story to Alan. Two years earlier, David had been invited to party in a friend's apartment. He could not smoke inside, because his friend did not like the smell of cigarettes. Nevertheless, David managed to convince his friend to smoke out an open window. His apartment was on the third floor. David drank a lot that night and smoked weed while sitting on the windowsill. After his tenth beer and third joint, he fell off the window. The fall injured his spine and he remained paralyzed from the waist down. David said:

DAVID    - So, that's how I became a crippled and now I want to commit suicide.

ALAN     - And how do you plan to do that?

DAVID    - I've already tried, but it didn't work... I've tried taking pills several times but I wake up every time. I want to hang myself but I can't fix the rope alone, because I am in a wheel chair.

ALAN     - Why don't you shoot yourself in the head?

DAVID    - I want to but I can't find a gun. We're not in the States... Guns are illegal here. My family is following me all the time to prevent me from committing suicide.

Alan explained that his father was an expert in medical devices designed to induce euthanasia. He told David that he had studied suicide and death for a long time. As many scientists, James talked about his research studies all the time. He was passionate about the philosophical and scientific aspects of death. This subject also fascinated Alan. James taught him virtually everything he knew about the art of dying painlessly. Alan told David that he was not surprised that his suicide attempts had failed so far. After talking for an hour about the logistical problems that people encounter these days to commit suicide without guns, David smiled and said:

DAVID    - You know, Alan, I thought you were an asshole but I start to like you. There's no bullshit with you. My family tells me that life is worth living even if you're in a wheelchair. But they don't understand me. Why would you keep living if you can't even get it up?

ALAN     - I understand you.

DAVID    - After my accident, my girlfriend dumped me and I lost all my friends!

David's girlfriend left him a month after his accident. She told him that she was too young to stay with a guy she could not have sex with. David's friends visited him at the hospital in the beginning. However, they contacted him less frequently when they fully realized the burden of his handicap. After some time, they only communicated through Facebook and avoided to have face-to-face interactions with him. David's friends gradually became virtual Facebook friends he never saw. After months of social isolation, David wanted to end his life using sleeping pills but it did not work. Following his first suicide attempt, the only thing that mattered to his family was to prevent him from committing suicide again. They did not understand David's persistent will to die.

DAVID — My family never listens to me. You're the first person who understands me since I had my accident.

ALAN — You want to die and I respect your choice. You feel alone because no one understands that you like sex more than life.

DAVID — Exactly, no one but you.

ALAN — How old are you?

DAVID — 25.

ALAN — 25. Interesting. And what do you do for a living?

DAVID    - Nothing... I receive money from the state, because I am disabled. I also come from a rich, Jewish family.

ALAN     - Oh, I see. So, money is not an issue for you?

DAVID    - No.

ALAN     - Do you believe in God?

DAVID    - I've stopped believing since my accident.

ALAN     - Perfect. I already know you like alcohol. But do you like drugs?

DAVID    - I love doing drugs.

ALAN     - Excellent. Why don't you come to the States with us?

DAVID    - Why? Will you give me a gun?

David laughed as he said that last sentence. He had not laughed since his accident.

ALAN     - I will prove to you that life is worth living two more years, even if you're an impotent crippled!

A couple of days later, Alan, David and his friends went back to the United States. David became the oldest member of the club. He also became Alan's friend because they shared common interests in philosophy and hedonism.

# CHAPTER 8
## HOW DAVID LEARNED
## TO BE HAPPY AGAIN IN SPITE
## OF HIS HANDICAP

David's life found a new meaning in the club and he relearned to enjoy all the simple pleasures that friendship can offer. He had always feared that he would become an old, lonely crippled. The idea of living alone several decades in his wheelchair terrified him. That all changed radically after he met Alan. He knew deep down that his new American friends were as shallow as his friends from France. They were just following Alan, the leader of their club, who happened to like him. However, David did not care, because he would be gone in two years. He wanted to make the best of a weird situation.

David started to do crack cocaine with Alan, a drug he had never tried before. They often smoked together and talked about philosophy for hours. In one of their conversations, David wanted to know why Alan created his club. He asked:

DAVID  - Why did you create a club restricted to young people? Why do you want to end your life so early? You have it all: the money, the looks, the girls...

ALAN - No one has it all. I am just like everyone else. I have a disease: I am aging. People of the twenty-first century don't wanna age and they waste all their lives trying to remain young: they quit smoking, they watch their diet, they spend all their time in the gym... In the process, they don't live. I want to live. I prefer a short fun life to a boring long one.

DAVID - Me too... What you just said reminds me of someone... Who said this?

ALAN - You probably mean Alexander the Great. He said, "I would rather live a short life of glory than a long one of obscurity."

DAVID - I see why you didn't quote him word for word. [said David laughing] Your life isn't exactly a life of glory! Your life is absurd!

ALAN - Yes, I know that. That's why I would rather have a short absurd life than a long absurd one.

DAVID - By the way, at what age did Alexander the Great die?

ALAN - 32. His life was actually not so short at that time...

DAVID - But it was a great life. Most people will live long, boring lives in weak, old bodies these days... My family doesn't get that I have to spend that long, boring life in a wheelchair…

ALAN    - People are not rational when it comes to aging and life. We all secretly yearn for a life where we stay young forever. We all subconsciously acknowledge that old age sucks. But most people are incapable of doing something about it. I am not part of them. How many times have you heard people saying that after college, the best years of your life are over?

DAVID    - Yeah, I heard people saying that in Europe.

ALAN    - People think that there is a weird, natural order that obligates them to grow old. That's just bullshit. In an atheist world, we can end our lives when we want. We have the right technology to do it. There's no God to tell us that it's morally wrong.

DAVID    - The right technology? How can we be sure that the FAPS-ROOM is 100% reliable?

ALAN    - It has always worked so far.

DAVID    - We should test the FAPS-ROOM.

ALAN    - I've already tried it with a chicken.

DAVID    - A chicken? Why a chicken?

ALAN    - Have you ever tried to shoot in the head of a chicken flying in every corner of a room? If you can shoot a chicken, you can shoot a human being.

DAVID   - Ok, I see what you mean… The FAPS-ROOM is a very flexible machine that can shoot in the head of a chicken… Does this mean that the FAPS-ROOM can recognize the target?

ALAN   - Yes, the FAPS-ROOM is a smart robot that can distinguish a human from an animal. It can recognize the head and the different parts of the body.

DAVID   - That's fucking amazing! But how do you know that the FAPS-ROOM aimed at the head of the chicken? It could hit the target by shooting randomly in every direction.

ALAN   - There's a screen outside the FAPS-ROOM that you can use to monitor what happens inside the room. The chicken was shot many times in the head, the neck and the heart. It's as if the head of the chicken disappeared instantly but the reclining chair remained intact because it wasn't in the line of fire. Then the remains of the chicken were collected by artificial arms and cremated.

DAVID   - If shooting in the head is so effective, why are so many people using lethal injections to execute criminals or to induce euthanasia?

ALAN   - Because there's no bloody corpse to take care of. Most people are frightened by the sight of blood. That's probably why my father robotized the entire killing procedure of his FAPS-ROOM, from the shooting to the cremation...

DAVID    - And once I am dead, will you organize a funeral?

ALAN    - No.

DAVID    - Why not?

ALAN    - Because it's more rational to organize a deathday party to honor someone's life.

DAVID    - I see... That's why deathday parties are so important in your club...

ALAN    - Yes, a deathday party makes more sense than a funeral. We should take care of our loved ones when they are still alive. Why should we waste our time for someone who can't benefit from his funeral if we can make him happy during his deathday party?

DAVID    - I don't know why... Maybe our society doesn't want to see death for what it really is: the end of an absurd life that was probably not worth living in the first place.

ALAN    - Not worth living? Who said that life is not worth living?

DAVID    - I think like you: life is not worth living. Don't you wanna kill yourself?

ALAN    - Yeah but I think life is worth living.

DAVID    - How can you think that life is worth living if you wanna commit suicide?

ALAN    - It's very simple: many philosophers asked themselves the wrong question. They wondered whether humans should commit suicide. However, the fundamental existential question is not "Should we commit suicide?" but "*When* should we commit suicide?"

DAVID    - What do you mean?

ALAN    - Of course, we should commit suicide in a FAPS-ROOM because natural deaths caused by cancer or degenerative diseases are more painful. Since we cannot escape death, we have be logical: we must choose a painless suicide over a painful deadly disease. But that doesn't mean that we can't enjoy our lives before our suicide.

DAVID    - Thus, you mean that life can be worth living for a certain period of time... The fundamental question is not "To be or not to be?" but rather "How long should we be?"

ALAN    - That is perfectly correct.

DAVID    - That does make sense... I wish my parents were as logical as you are.

Alan and David continued to talk about the irrational opinions most people have about life, suicide and death. David was glad, because he had finally met a friend with whom he could talk about his existential problems without being judged.

After the terrible accident that left him crippled, David completely lost his appetite, because he suffered from a severe depression. His appetite slowly came back after he arrived in the USA and he enjoyed eating again. Alan made sure that he could find all the best French food he liked. After a few months, David ate excessively during meals that lasted at least two hours every day. During these long meals, he was drunk and happy and talked about sex all the time. He loved to tell indecent French jokes to shock his American friends. However, it was very difficult to offend the members of Alan's club and they usually played the game and reciprocated with even more obscene jokes. David gained a lot of weight and it became more and more difficult to carry him from his wheelchair to his bed and vice versa. Alan hired two new nurses for him. David's alcohol consumption also increased; he usually drank five bottles of Bordeaux every day. Moreover, he used heroin on a regular basis. He was high most of the time and stopped being obsessed with his handicap. He lived in an artificial dream and spent all his money on food, alcohol and drugs.

# CHAPTER 9
## HOW DAVID, JACK AND JENNY DIED

When David's twenty-eighth birthday was approaching, he could hardly believe that he would die in peace and never have to deal with his handicap again. He was much happier than two years earlier but knew that his life in America was completely artificial. If he left the club to go back to France, he realized that he would be miserable again. If he decided to stay alive, he knew that he would have to deal with his drug problems and change his eating habits that made him very fat. David needed high amounts of heroin, alcohol and food to feel good. He knew deep down that he had become an obese, alcoholic junkie. It did not matter anymore, since he would be a dead, obese, alcoholic junkie very soon. He said to Alan:

DAVID    - I am not afraid to die. There must be a catch but I can't put my finger on it. It seems too easy!

ALAN    - It seems easy thanks to the FAPS-ROOM that will do all the dirty work for us. Without the FAPS-ROOM, you would be scared to death. We would have to deal with difficult logistic problems: how to induce death painlessly and effectively, how to dispose of your body...

DAVID - Maybe there's no catch after all. Maybe humans can decide when they end their lives with the right technology.

ALAN - There is only one catch: you go to hell, because suicide is a sin. [said Alan ironically]

Alan and David laughed, because neither of them believed in an afterlife. The next day, the members of the club started to plan David's deathday party. They ordered David's favorite food, his favorite bottles of wine and Champagne. Alan also hired three prostitutes that David found attractive and funny. A week before the deathday party, Alan wanted to be sure that David still wanted to die. He said:

ALAN - Are you sure you want to end your life in the FAPS-ROOM? You can also go back to France.

DAVID - I lived two decent years thanks to you. If I return to France, my life will be as miserable as two years ago. Let's get this over with!

ALAN - Thus, you are absolutely sure that you want to disappear forever?

DAVID - Yes, I am sure. [replied David with an irritated voice]

ALAN    - One hundred percent sure??? I have to ask these questions at least three times. It's part of the guidelines of my club.

DAVID   - Yes, yes and yes. By the way, why do you always say "end your life" or "disappear"? You never say "commit suicide."

ALAN    - It's easier to process mentally. The philosophy of my club is that you don't commit suicide but you "disappear off the face of the earth with no questions asked." You leave planet Earth like you would leave a boring party.

DAVID   - But at the end of the day, you kill yourself.

ALAN    - Not really. You actually ask a robot to kill you. You don't do it yourself. And the FAPS-ROOM really makes you disappear. People will keep thinking you're alive. When you kill yourself with a gun for example, you don't disappear from a technical point of view. Your body is still there and is proof of your death.

DAVID   - But the FAPS-ROOM also causes death, which is painful... You inflict yourself pain... Isn't that difficult to reconcile with hedonism?

ALAN    - Not at all. Pain caused by death affects the hedonist's net pleasure only if death is painful but the FAPS-ROOM ends your life painlessly.

DAVID    - How do you know that the FAPS-ROOM causes no pain at all?

ALAN     - You need a brain to process pain signals but the FAPS-ROOM destroys the entire central nervous system at once. Moreover, you take painkillers before the shooting.

DAVID    - No pain at all? It seems too good to be true!

ALAN     - It is possible that the FAPS-ROOM causes some pain. We will never know. But there is nothing we can do about it. It's the best technology we have so far.

DAVID    - How can you be so sure?

ALAN     - I trust my father. He was an expert in thanatology.

DAVID    - Thanatology? What is thanatology?

ALAN     - It's the scientific study of death.

DAVID    - The science of death? Is that a real thing? Sometimes, I think you're just making things up to convince people to join your crazy club.

ALAN     - Look it up if you don't believe me. I love thanatology; it tells you so much about human nature.

David looked up thanatology on his smart phone and learned that it is a scientific discipline that really exists. He was reassured and said happily:

DAVID    - I think that I am ready to die! I can't believe that all I have to do is go into the

FAPS-ROOM and I will never have to worry about my handicap again!

ALAN — - We have to take care of some logistical problems first. We must make everyone believe you'll still be alive after using the FAPS-ROOM. How is your relationship with your parents?

DAVID — - Terrible, I never speak to them.

ALAN — - Perfect. When was the last time you saw your parents?

DAVID — - Two years ago.

ALAN — - We can text your parents once a month.

DAVID — - Oh, that's too much... I've texted them only three times since I've been in the States.

ALAN — - Once a year just on New Year's Eve?

DAVID — - That's plenty enough!

A week later, all the members of the club gathered in Alan's country house to celebrate David's deathday party. The evening started at 7 PM with aperitifs. Everyone drank a lot. David finished two bottles of Vermouth by himself. He then indulged in his favorite activity: eating like a pig. Appetizers were served and consisted of seafood: oysters, coquilles Saint-Jacques, lobster, salmon and caviar. David stuffed himself with all the caviar. A little bit later, he ate his favorite meal one last time. Roasted chicken was served with Gratin Dauphinois, braised peas and glazed carrots. David drank three bottles of Saint-Émilion and ate chicken and potatoes until he was sick. Then he vomited his meal and fell asleep. The members woke him up an hour later for the traditional European desserts: crème brûlée, chocolate mousse, Crêpe Suzette, tiramisu and sabayon. David ingested as much dessert as he could and ate all the tiramisu. At 9:30 PM, an orgy was organized, so David could indulge his sexual fantasies. When the prostitutes started to touch him below the waist, he felt absolutely nothing and realized how miserable his life would be if he returned to France. To change his mind, he continued to eat pancakes, drank more wine and snorted a lot of cocaine.

The suicide ceremony started at 11:10 PM sharp. Alan opened champagne bottles and everyone could drink *ad libitum.* All the members wished David a happy deathday and sang the happy deathday song, which was identical to the traditional birthday song except that "birthday" was replaced with "deathday." After the song, David said goodbye to each member individually. He had eaten and drunk so much that he could barely move. Then some members carried him into the FAPS-ROOM and put him in the reclining chair. David injected himself with a high dose of heroin. The members left the room and the FAPS-program asked David whether he was absolutely certain that he wanted to end his life. David said yes. A couple of minutes later, he fell asleep, sedated by heroin and alcohol. At 11:45 PM, Alan and his friends heard gunshots in the

FAPS-ROOM. The gunshots were barely audible but everyone knew exactly when David died. After midnight, Alan spread his ashes in the woods. Alan was sad that he lost his friend. In the meantime, he was relieved that David would no longer suffer in his wheelchair in France. Alan had saved David from his greatest fear: dying alone and miserably at an old age.

Alan was glad that the first deathday party was a success. Everything worked as planned. No one knew that David had died; there was no body and no evidence of David's suicide. Alan was convinced that his club was the logical answer to life's problems and injustices. The next day, Alan and his friends woke up completely hung over. At 3 PM, they went to the kitchen to eat breakfast. Louise had bought croissants and prepared eggs for everyone. Jack had terrible headaches because he had drunk four bottles of vodka the night before. He was sweating like a pig and was trembling a lot. At the age of 24, Jack was already a full-blown alcoholic and needed to drink to stop shaking. He opened a bottle of wine, drank from it and said:

JACK     - That's it? Is David dead?
JENNY   - Of course he's dead, idiot!
JACK     - You just enter a room and disappear. This machine is awesome. Death no longer seems like death. I wanna be next!
ALAN     - But you're too young... you have three years left...

JACK      - I can't stand it anymore. I need to drink
          all the time. I am a complete alcoholic. I
          am 24 and I pee all the time!

Alan and Jenny laughed. Humiliated, Jack left the kitchen and went to the basement. Alan said:

ALAN      - He's heading to the FAPS-ROOM on a
          whim! We have to stop him!

Several members of the club ran after Jack and prevented him from entering the FAPS-ROOM. Alan and Jenny tried to talk him out of using the FAPS-ROOM. Alan said:

ALAN      - You're just hung over. You've been
          shaking in the morning since you were
          20! Why do you want to kill yourself to-
          day?
JACK      - I want to get rid of my fucking head-
          aches!
ALAN      - Just take these pills, you will be fine in
          a couple of hours.

Alan gave Jack Ibuprofen and Xanax. He swallowed the pills and finished his bottle of wine. He returned to his bedroom and slept until 7 PM. When he woke up, he was still shaking and sweating. He drank a bottle of vodka and felt a little better. Then he wanted to leave the country house to change his mind. He took his old Porsche 911 and drove completely drunk on small roads at 90 miles per hour. He arrived on a long road that allowed him to accelerate to 150 miles per hour. Unfortunately, he drove too fast to negotiate a bend and lost control of his car. He drove into a big tree. Because he never wore his seat belt, his body flew through the windshield like a cannonball and hit the tree face-on. His face was unrecognizable but the features of his skull were engraved on the trunk of the tree. So, Jack died on the spot at the age of 24, only one day after David.

Jack's death terrorized all the members of the club. Alan made a little speech in Jack's honor in front of all the other members. Louise served glasses of wine to everyone. Alan encouraged the members to drink heavily to distract their minds from David and Jack's deaths. He said sadly:

ALAN    - Jack died like he always wanted to: he died on the spot, completely drunk in a car crash. Jack was the wildest of us all. I have always envied Jack for his ability to just live in the moment. Jack was the wisest of us all. He didn't need the fine logistics of my club. He reminds us that ignorance is bliss.

Alan raised his glass of wine and repeated:

ALAN    - Ignorance is bliss! To Jack!

And then all the other members raised their glasses and shouted together:

OTHERS - Ignorance is bliss! To Jack!

Alan drank his wine in one gulp and everyone did the same. Then he poured himself another glass of wine and so did the other members. He raised his glass and said:

ALAN    - We love you Jack! Ignorance is bliss!

And he drank his wine in one gulp. The members kept imitating Alan. He poured another glass and said:

ALAN    - This one is for David! To David! Down the hatch!

OTHERS - To David, down the hatch!

And everyone kept drinking and partying. Everyone was completely drunk, drunker than usual. Two members were so intoxicated that they went into a coma. Fortunately, Louise was sober enough to drive them to the hospital at the right time. Miraculously, no one died that night.

Life continued in the club with its endless parties of debauchery. Alan and his friends traveled a lot. They went to Stockholm, Prague, Zermatt, Berlin, Dortmund, Brighton, London (three times), Dublin, Paris (eleven times), Lisbon, Barcelona, Rome (twice), Venice, Corfu, Cluj-Napoca, Istanbul, Moscow (twice), Carthage, Cairo, Giza, Kinshasa, Cape Town, Shanghai, Hong Kong, Tokyo, Sydney, Tahiti, Mexico City (twice), Paramaribo, Rio de Janeiro, Asunción, Buenos Aires and Esperanza Base; all places where Alan could indulge his passion for sex with women from different cultures. They came back to the US when a member was about to turn 28 and chose to use the FAPS-ROOM.

Jenny died in a tragic accident during a deathday party. While under the influence of LSD, she was convinced that she was a turkey and wanted to fly. She went to the kitchen of the country house and detached a shelf from the wall. The shelf was a long, wooden plank. Jenny had the crazy idea to use it as a ramp to help her fly. Then she went to the balcony of the fourth floor of the country house, which was very large. She placed one end of the wooden plank on the floor of the balcony and the other end on the balustrade. Then she ran as fast as she could on the plank and jumped off the balcony. For a short while, Jenny certainly had the IQ of a turkey but she did not fly. She fell on a marble statue representing an angel that stood in the yard. The fall did not kill her but her spine was severely damaged at the level of the neck. Because she would remain quadriplegic for the rest of her life, her friends did not call an ambulance but dragged her body into the FAPS-ROOM. That's where she died at the age of 25.

# CHAPTER 10
## HOW ALAN DIED

When Alan turned 27, he complained about several health problems caused by his depraved lifestyle. He was now a full-blown alcoholic completely addicted to heroin. He suffered from chronic constipation and he coughed a lot. Moreover, he had erection problems. He called a physician for this and invited him to his country house. The consultation happened in the living room. Alan was sitting lazily in a large leather couch smoking a cigarette and he proposed one to the doctor who said:

DOCTOR- Thanks, I don't smoke. Why did you want to see me?

ALAN     - I've called you because I can't get it up.

DOCTOR- And when did you start having erection problems?

ALAN     - A week ago.

DOCTOR- I see,... and how old are you?

ALAN     - 27.

DOCTOR- 27?! Really?? [said the doctor surprised]

ALAN     - Yeah, why? [said Alan laughing]

DOCTOR- You look older. I thought you were in your mid-thirties. I can't believe that you're younger than me.... What's your job?

ALAN    - Technically, I am a philosopher but I've never worked a single day in my life. [said Alan proudly]

DOCTOR- Why??

ALAN    - I've inherited my father's fortune. I have enough money until I die.

DOCTOR- You're a parasite! This is a real shame.

ALAN    - I serve society by not working.

DOCTOR- How?

ALAN    - It's very simple: very rich people help the poor by not working. Automation and robotics destroy many jobs. So, everyone competes for the few jobs that are left. If I choose to work, someone who really needs a job becomes unemployed and eventually homeless.

The doctor remained silent for three seconds and finally said:

DOCTOR- That actually makes sense...

ALAN    - Imagine that all the rich people who can easily get jobs because they know the right people decided to stop working. A lot of poor people could find jobs.

DOCTOR- Yes, but you're only right because our society is completely fucked up...

ALAN    - But that's not my fault. At the end of the day, I do a good deed when I decide to be lazy. I am more useful to society when I don't work than when I work.

DOCTOR- I must admit that you have a very logical mind. Did you go to college?

ALAN    - Yes.

DOCTOR- What did you study?

ALAN    - Nothing. I go to college to party, to meet more women...

DOCTOR- Don't you think that smart people like you should do something with their lives? With your rational mind, you could become an engineer or a computer scientist.

ALAN    - Really? [said Alan laughing] To invent more robots and increase unemployment rates even more? Computer scientists are destroying jobs. Thanks to my lazy lifestyle, I create many jobs. I employ one accountant, one house keeper, five maids, one chauffeur, two nurses and one secretary.

The doctor could not help laughing.

DOCTOR- To figure out why you have erection problems, I need to ask you other questions. Do you smoke a lot?

ALAN    - Yes.

DOCTOR- How much?

ALAN    - Three packs a day.

DOCTOR- Three packs a day? Smoking so much can cause erectile dysfunction. You must either quit smoking or smoke less.

DOCTOR- Do you drink alcohol?

ALAN    - Yes.

DOCTOR- How much?

ALAN    - It's very difficult to tell. I drink beer and wine every day. I drink a lot of tequila and vodka.

DOCTOR- What happens when you don't drink?

ALAN    - I shake, I sweat,... I feel terrible...

DOCTOR- You might be an alcoholic.

ALAN    - You can tell me that I am an alcoholic. I know that.

DOCTOR- Do you take drugs?

ALAN    - Heroin on a daily basis, I also smoke pot and crack cocaine. I take LSD, methamphetamine, MDMA and every other psychoactive drug that is available.

DOCTOR- No wonder that you can't get it up...

The physician examined Alan and concluded that his erection problems were caused by his excessive use of tobacco, alcohol and drugs. He advised Alan to go to rehab and quit all drugs. He told him that he should not quit everything at the same time. First, he should quit drugs and alcohol over several months. Then he should quit smoking. The doctor explained that, because Alan was a polydrug addict, it would take him several months to become completely clean and see an improvement in his sex life. Alan said that he would follow his advice and asked for a Viagra prescription. The doctor prescribed him Viagra.

Alan never went to rehab and continued to lead his depraved lifestyle. When his twenty-eighth birthday was approaching, he was excited to leave this world, because his health problems were getting worse and his drug use was out of control. He suffered from erectile dysfunction even after taking Viagra. He had the face of a man in his late thirties but his body was less efficient than most people in their fifties. Alan thought that it was ridiculous to keep living if he could not have an erection and he was eager to die in his FAPS-ROOM. When he turned 27 years and 364 days old, the members of his club organized an awesome deathday party to celebrate his departure. To have sex one last time, Alan swallowed all the Viagra pills he could find. He died of a heart attack shortly after.

After his death, Alan's spirit was transferred to an unknown location, somewhere in the galaxy. An old, handsome guy with a long, white beard started to talk:

GOD     - Case Alan Henry Donovan.

ALAN    - That's me, what's happening? I am supposed to be dead. Where am I?

GOD     - Your case will be easy to handle. Since your desire was to never grow old, your spirit will be transferred in an immortal jelly fish.

ALAN    - Oh come on? You exist!? Can't you just send me to hell!!

GOD      - No, you need the free will to act immor-
          ally to go to hell. You sold your free will
          for one thousand dollars. The person
          who bought your free will tricked you
          into creating your immoral secret soci-
          ety. Terry Bradfield is the real founder of
          your club. You're punished for having
          wasted my most precious gift to you:
          your free will.
ALAN     - Free will exists?
GOD      - As long as you believe in it.
ALAN     - That's interesting… Thus, the very fact
          of not believing in free will makes it dis-
          appear…
GOD      - That's right.

Alan could not believe that the entire philosophical system he had imagined was completely
wrong. In a last attempt to escape his pathetic
fate, he tried to bargain with God to be reincar-
nated in an animal more evolved than a jellyfish.
He said:

ALAN     - By the way, God… I don't wanna be too
          technical but my father taught me that
          lobsters don't age. Since my desire was to
          never grow old, shouldn't I be a lobster
          instead of a jelly fish?
GOD      - I don't want to be too technical either,
          but lobsters eventually die despite they
          don't age. Thus, they can't remain eter-
          nally young from a technical point of

view. Nice try, Alan. But I've decided that you're a jellyfish.

ALAN    - Who's Terry Bradfield?

Alan suddenly heard a voice whispering softly:

SATAN   - My dear, naive servant, do you still ignore the name of your master?

Alan could not locate where the whisper was coming from but he recognized Terry Bradfield's voice. He finally understood the satanic nature of the club he believed to have founded.

GOD     - Never listen to him again. He's not your master anymore. I grant you another free will. You're a jelly fish now! Next case!

ALAN    - Just like that?

And Alan's spirit was reborn in a jellyfish, just like that. He was reborn in *Turritopsis dohrnii*, a species of jellyfish that has the ability to revert to its polyp stage under certain conditions. The jellyfish grows in multiple phases. The larva is the first stage and develops into a polyp before becoming an adult jellyfish. The polyp looks like a small cylinder with tentacles (Figure 2B). When *Turritopsis dohrnii* is constantly kept under the right circumstances, it reverts endlessly to its polyp stage and becomes immortal (Figure 2).

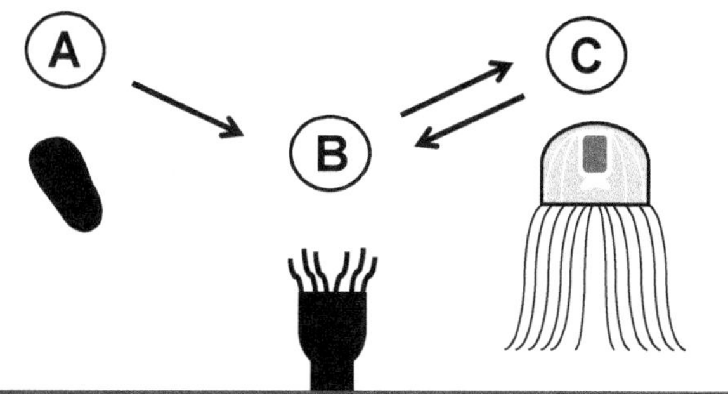

Figure 2. How Alan became biologically immortal. The jellyfish develops into multiple phases. Larva is the first stage (A). The larva attaches itself to a solid surface and develops into a polyp (B). Then the polyp transforms into an adult jellyfish (C). When *Turritopsis dohrnii* is constantly kept under the right circumstances, it reverts endlessly to its polyp stage and becomes biologically immortal.

Alan lived in a colony of jellyfish that belonged to a famous Japanese scientist named Dr. Hiroshimato Sato, who studied immortality. Scientists put him in a tiny, transparent bottle to examine his development. Alan never grew old and never worked a single day, exactly like he always wanted to. He had all the time he wanted to ponder about the human condition and become the philosopher he pretended to be in his previous life. Several decades later, Dr. Hiroshimato Sato was awarded the Nobel Prize in Physiology or

Medicine for his discovery of the cure for aging. Humans made other important scientific breakthroughs during the third millennium. They invented intelligent humanoid robots. They improved their fully automated companies and made a lot of progress in medicine and neurosciences. The wealthiest people benefited from the medical techniques for the treatment of aging. Moreover, their intelligence was enhanced by nanotechnological devices allowing constant direct brain Internet access. Intelligent robots performed most of the work. As a result, the majority of people lost their jobs and lived in extreme poverty. They continued to die of age-related diseases because they could not afford to pay for the biotechnology that provided youth and health.

From his bottle, Alan witnessed the three major breakthroughs of the third millennium that changed the world forever: intelligent humanoid robots, brain Internet and the cure for aging. In his jellyfish life, he remained an idealistic creature but was less selfish than during his human life. Now able to distinguish good from evil, Alan used his analytical mind to imagine a better world in which scientific and technological progress would benefit to every human being. Alan considered that artificial intelligence, brain Internet and the cure for aging could be beneficial to mankind only if three major socio-economic and philosophical changes occur in parallel: the systematic sharing of some money, the universal provision of a free, high-quality education and the responsible use of FAPS-ROOMs. Alan imagined three practical antidotes to the three major breakthroughs of the third millennium.

In the third millennium, intelligent humanoid robots and artificial intelligence reduced the need to hire people and pay them to work. As a result, many people could not find work and had no money. Partially dissociating work from income seemed inevitable to solve the problem of poverty in this dystopian world. Therefore, Alan imagined a practical economic system that allowed humans to receive a certain amount of money even if their jobs were taken over by intelligent robots. In his economic system, all the banks of the world were merged into a unique international bank that stored and redistributed money to every citizen of the world on a monthly basis. A single currency was used worldwide, called the Doro. The Doro was a form of smart currency that could be tracked by the international banking system through Global Positioning System (GPS). The Doro currency consisted in material coins and bills that incorporated nanotechnology allowing GPS location. A bank account was opened for every citizen of the world, through which he received a basic income every month from birth to death. This universal basic income (UBI) was unconditional. This meant that every human being received it automatically unless he deliberately and actively refused it. The universal basic income was high enough to allow every human to fulfill his needs and live in dignity. However, this basic income was fixed by the market to remain low enough to motivate people to keep working.

To prevent corruption, Alan imagined an international banking system that was fully automated. It could work without human intervention and could accurately track the total number of citizens in the world and the total amount of Doros. In other words, every Doro was tracked whether it was in the bank or not. Because the universal basic income was not mandatory, rich people had the possibility to actively refuse their universal basic income every month. The first priority of Alan's fully automated banking system was to provide the universal basic income to everyone. To reach that objective, it automatically removed a precise amount of money from the highest fortunes if money was missing to provide basic incomes. This feedback mechanism was essential to ensure that the universal basic income was delivered every month to everyone despite economic fluctuations.

Alan believed that a free, high-quality education in English should be the right of all the children in the world. He thought that all humans should share at least one common language to be able to understand each other's cultural differences and live peacefully. Alan wanted to promote the teaching of philosophy, history, sciences, environmental ethics and the use of new technologies. A high-quality education was an antidote to the potential problems caused by artificial intelligence (AI) and a constant access to the Internet that could lead to psychological disorders and online addiction. Guaranteeing a free education to everyone was also a healthy way to keep people busy and create a lot of jobs, whether they were paid or not.

Alan imagined a world in which each human being could benefit from the cure for aging. His father's invention found its place in this new world. The FAPS-ROOM replaced the aging process that allowed life to end. It was the antidote to the boredom and alienation that could potentially result from an indefinite lifespan. In addition, the FAPS-ROOM could prevent overpopulation in a world where people no longer died from aging.

Instead of reminding people that they should fight for their right to keep smoking in bars, Alan wanted to advocate more noble ideas in his jellyfish life. He imagined six fundamental human/transhuman rights that allowed humanity to function properly as long as these rights were fully respected. His six human rights were based on the major breakthroughs of the third millennium and the three antidotes he had imagined. Alan formulated his fundamental rights in such a way that they balanced each other to allow society to function harmoniously on a theoretical level (see Table 1, page 126). Unfortunately, no one knew about his idealistic ideas, since he was just a jellyfish trapped in a bottle. That was good enough for God, who eventually released his soul from eternal boredom.

<u>Table 1. The six fundamental human/transhuman
rights of the third millennium by Alan Donovan</u>

| Major breakthrough | Antidote |
| --- | --- |
| **Intelligent humanoid robots**<br><br>*I. Every human is free and has the right to do what he chooses as long as he respects the law and does not harm other humans. Robots serve all mankind and deliver every human from undesired jobs and from all forms of slavery.* | **Universal basic income delivered by a fully automated international bank**<br><br>*II. Every human deserves an income, high enough to fulfill his needs and live in dignity whether he works or not.* |
| **Brain Internet and instant access to knowledge**<br><br>*III. Every human has the right to access to knowledge through the Internet and benefit from the nanotechnology that enhances intelligence.* | **Universal high-quality education**<br><br>*IV. Every human deserves a free, high-quality education to be warned against the potential dangers of AI and the constant use of the Internet.* |
| **The cure for aging**<br><br>*V. Every human has the right to benefit from the biotechnology that provides youth and health.* | **FAPS-ROOM**<br><br>*VI. Every human has the right to die in dignity and painlessly.* |

*Work saves us from three great evils:*
*need, vice and boredom.*

*Le travail éloigne de nous trois grands maux :*
*le besoin, le vice et l'ennui.*

Voltaire (Candide, 1759).

# The Diabolic Recipe
for True Love

Imagine that a small community of very tiny dwarfs lives hidden from human society since the dawn of time. Imagine that their job is to guide the souls of humans through the spiritual world after their deaths on Earth. Imagine that they really exist, just for a while. The dwarfs are connected to the afterlife and play an important role in Destiny. Most dwarfs are good and faithfully assist God. Unfortunately, some dwarfs are evil and love to mess with God's plans. Their job is to keep humans on Earth for as long as possible in order to make them suffer more, until they die alone and miserably of old age. Each evil dwarf has a birthmark on his chest shaped like the astronomical symbol of Saturn[2]. No one knows that there are evil dwarfs in the community, because

---

[2] For the readers who have not read the previous Saturnian Tales, the astronomical symbol of Saturn is represented in black on the book cover, between the star and the pyramid. In addition, the symbolism of Saturn is explained in the fourth chapter of FAPS-ROOM (first paragraph), the second Saturnian Tale.

they usually act very cunningly so that nothing except their birthmark can reveal their Machiavellian nature.

To understand how the dwarfs operate on a cosmic level, I will tell you a little story that happened in the twenty-first century about the dwarfs from the state of Illinois. For centuries, the Illinoisan dwarfs lived in a big oak that stood along a small road in the woods. They left the tree exclusively to do their job or to find mushrooms, their only diet. At the beginning of the twenty-first century, the Illinoisan dwarfs had to handle the case of two eighteen-year-old high school sweethearts who were involved in a terrible car accident: Brian Smith and Janis Conway. They had met each other in high school and had fallen in love at the age of fourteen. Since then, Brian and Janis loved each other passionately until the car accident that happened at the end of their senior year.

On prom night, Brian was completely drunk and could not take his car to drive to his place. So, Janis took Brian's car and drove him to her home. She still lived with her parents and planned to let Brian sleep over. It was already past midnight when she started to drive and there was a big storm. Janis took her cell phone to call her mother. She wanted to tell her that she would be home late. Suddenly, Brian vomited on Janis and she lost control of the car. The car skidded off the wet road and crashed into a tree. Neither Brian nor Janis wore their seat belt and their heads banged the windshield. They were both unconscious and lost a lot of blood. Unfortunately, no one was there to help them. The accident happened near the oak of the Illinoisan dwarfs. Humans were rarely present in that area after midnight, especially during a storm. So the dwarfs were the only ones to witness the accident. Their names were Wimpy, Witty, Cheesy, Sleazy and Sloppy. Wimpy was afraid of everything, even of talking. Witty was always rational and logical. Cheesy was caring and emotional most of the time. Sleazy was an evil dwarf and Sloppy was the boss.

It was still raining heavily when the dwarfs arrived near the accident scene. Witty had paperwork in the right hand and an umbrella in the left one. He whispered to the other dwarfs:

WITTY   - Names: Brian Smith and Janis Conway. They are high school sweethearts and are dying.

CHEESY - I love these cases. So easy to handle! Their love is so pure. They deserve the "true love" label.

SLOPPY - Seems fair to me. We wait for their deaths and we can fill out the paperwork and send their souls to God. I am sure he will agree on the "true love" label and they will be sent to the highest district of Paradise.

SLEAZY - Not so fast! It's not necessarily true love. They are not dead yet. You know the protocol: we have to help them as long as no one can prove that we interfere with Destiny.

SLOPPY - But what can we do?

CHEESY - And why should we intervene? Their love story can only deteriorate. You all know how it ends when humans grow old. The magic of true love vanishes forever after the first Saturn return.

SLEAZY - Just do your job.

The evil dwarf searched the couple's car and found Janis's cell phone. Her mother's number appeared on the screen. He pressed the call button. The evil dwarf whispered to the other dwarfs:

SLEAZY - The cell phone fell during the crash and the call button could have been pressed accidentally.

WITTY - Makes sense to me.

Five seconds later, Janis's mother picked up the phone and the dwarfs could hear her:

MOTHER - Hello?... Hello?... Janis, do you hear me?

Janis was unconscious and did not hear her mother. Janis's mother realized that something was wrong and said to her husband:

MOTHER - There must be something wrong with Janis. She called me but she didn't say anything on the phone. She should already be home by now. I will drive to the prom.

On her way to the prom, Janis's mother saw Brian's car crashed into a tree. She called an ambulance that arrived 20 minutes later.

Brian and Janis had lost a lot of blood but the ambulance arrived on time. They were rushed to the hospital and their lives were saved. Janis fully recuperated from the accident three months later. Brian's spine was badly injured and he remained paralyzed from the waist down. He could no longer have sex. Janis started cheating on him with a young doctor she met at the hospital. The evil dwarf whispered to the others:

SLEAZY  - Told you! It's not true love.

WITTY   - But it could have been true love if they had died. They are still together. One mistake under tragic circumstances is understandable. We need to wait for their deaths to make that assumption.

Ten years after the accident, Brian and Janis broke up because she had started dating the doctor. Brian never found a job. He became seriously depressed and tried to commit suicide at the age of 30. Unable to find a firearm, Brian stabbed himself in the stomach with a butcher knife in order to end his life. Then he fell on the floor and cried in agony. His neighbor heard his screams of pain and entered Brian's apartment. When the neighbor found him covered in blood lying on the floor, he called 911 right away and the ambulance arrived 30 minutes later. Brian was rushed to the hospital at the right time and survived. Because he was severely injured, he had to stay in the hospital for several months to recover completely. His room was on the fourth floor. One night of January, he managed to open a window and fell off it in another attempt to end his life. The next morning, the nurses found his body lying in the snow. There were five inches of snow that day. Brian survived his fall but became paralyzed from the neck down. He could no longer move and was unable to commit suicide again. He died of cancer at the age of 78. The Illinoisan dwarfs had to handle Brian's case in the afterlife. Sloppy and Cheesy were very upset. They realized that Brian's destiny had been changed for the worse, because of a single button press on a cell phone.

SLOPPY - I can't believe the story of Brian's life! He lived happily for eighteen years and was miserable during the next 60 years.

CHEESY - We never should have made that damned call! He was so close to finding true love!

SLEAZY - Told you! It was not true love. If Janis and Brian had truly loved each other, Janis would have stayed with him despite his handicap. True love overcomes accidents and tragedies.

CHEESY - That's bullshit! You know they truly loved each other before the accident.

SLOPPY   - No, he's right Cheesy. They didn't truly love each other. There was no tragedy to prove it.

SLEAZY   - You know God's rules: true love is eternal and must therefore last until death on Earth. If it does not, it was not true love. After death, the souls become soul mates and are bound together in the afterlife and this is what makes true love eternal.

CHEESY   - I hate God's rules! But it makes sense... and it's so romantic...

SLEAZY   - So what? Brian's soul won't be sent to the highest district of Paradise. Why do you care?

CHEESY   - I know... but they were so close. It's so rare now. In the past, so many people found true love.

WITTY    - What do you expect? The average life span of the human being is so long now that you can virtually spoil every relationship. There's always someone with a cell phone to call an ambulance when there's an accident. Therefore, people rarely die in accidents nowadays. Moreover, medical sciences are so advanced that it's very unlikely to die of a disease before old age. People in the twenty-first century die slowly and gradually of age-related diseases after they retire: cancer, cardiovascular diseases, Alzheimer's disease, even though patients actually don't die of Alzheimer's but from the complications of this disease.

Witty loved to lecture the other dwarfs with his boring scientific knowledge. Fortunately, the evil dwarf hated nerds and stopped Witty:

SLEAZY - Shut up Witty! You can still find true love. The trick is to die right after someone you love says "I love you" back. With a loaded gun and good timing, you can still make it to the highest district of Paradise.

This statement shocked the other dwarfs. They did not know how to react. For a moment, no one spoke. They were looking at each other, hoping that someone would break the silence. The pressure was so intense that Wimpy started to cry. Then the evil dwarf continued to speak:

SLEAZY - Oh, come on! Don't be so shocked, you're a bunch of hypocrites! You all know God's rules. If you don't like guns, a FAPS-ROOM can also do the trick[3]. I heard that they were designed for couples.

---

[3] For the readers who have not read the second Saturnian Tale, a FAPS-ROOM is a medical robot especially designed to assist people in dying instantly and painlessly. The medical robot is described in the second chapter of FAPS-ROOM, the second Saturnian Tale.

CHEESY - Why is God so technical about the rules of love?! I can't believe Adolf Hitler married Eva Braun right before committing suicide just to secure one of the best spots in heaven! Who taught him the trick?

SLEAZY - I did. [said the evil dwarf with a smirk on his face]

CHEESY - Seriously?

SLEAZY - Noooh!!! I am just messing with you. It was a coincidence. They got married because they knew they had lost the war.

SLOPPY - Where do we send Brian's soul?

SLEAZY - Brian had a pathetic life. Let's send him to the lowest district of Paradise.

WITTY - Makes sense to me: a pathetic district for a pathetic life.

CHEESY - Come on guys! Brian was a nice guy. There are some districts in Hell that are more fun than the lowest district of Paradise.

SLEAZY - Yes, as you say, Brian was a nice guy. That's exactly why he won't be sent to the cool districts of Hell.

Janis was still alive after Brian's death. She went to his funeral with her husband. Her life was not as pathetic as Brian's. She went to college and got a Master of Business Administration. She married the doctor she met at the hospital. Seven years later, the doctor dumped her for a younger woman. Then Janis dated different guys. At 42, she settled down with a guy named Patrick. She married him and wanted to raise a family. However, she could no longer be pregnant. So she focused on her career until the age of 65. Thirteen years later, a month after Brian's death, Janis was diagnosed with Alzheimer's disease. Immediately after the diagnosis, Patrick sent her to a nursing home and managed to live with an ex-girlfriend who had become a widow. Patrick never visited Janis. She died alone at the age of 93 in a hospital. After her death, the Illinoisan dwarfs debated Janis's fate in the afterlife:

CHEESY - Patrick was a real ass! He really did not care about Janis. He did not love her.

WITTY  - Forget the highest district. From her file, it looks like she should be sent to an intermediate district of Paradise.

SLEAZY - She cheated on Brian. I see on her file that she was a slut in her thirties. She should go to one of the nasty districts of Hell.

SLOPPY - Really??? You want to send her with criminals and murderers while Hitler is in the highest district of Paradise? Janis was a good, ordinary person.

SLEAZY - Maybe Hell is too harsh. We could ask God to reincarnate her in a pig.

SLOPPY - Sometimes Sleazy,... Sometimes, I wonder if I really know you. You just fill out the paper work but you don't care that souls that were connected on Earth roam alone forever in the afterlife.

SLEAZY - She can still find true love on a farm.

SLOPPY - Forget the pig reincarnation idea.

SLEAZY - Ok, you made your point. We will send Janis's soul to an intermediate district of Paradise.

Witty was about to complete the form of Janis. The evil dwarf handed him the pen and said smiling:

SLEAZY - Just sign and let's get this over with!

But Cheesy had suddenly another idea and took the form off Witty's hands:

CHEESY - You know what Witty? We will not follow the protocol blindly this time: Janis's soul should be transferred to the lowest district of Paradise. Maybe it's not the one she deserves based on her record but it's the one where there's still hope for her.

WITTY - You expect that Janis's soul finds Brian's. I know you mean well but it is almost impossible that they will meet each other: the lowest district of Paradise is the largest and the most crowded. Janis won't even know that Brian is in the same district.

After a long discussion, the dwarfs finally agreed on Cheesy's cheesy idea. Janis's degenerated soul was transferred to the lowest, lamest and most annoying district of Paradise, just near the borders of Hell. Her soul roamed alone and erratically in the afterlife for a very long time. There was nothing in the lowest district of Paradise except yellowish-green grass and damaged, lonely souls for thousands of miles. The odds of finding a particular roaming soul were very slim. Fortunately, the crippled and depressed soul of Brian had not moved an inch since it was transferred to the lowest district of Paradise. After wandering randomly for several centuries, Janis's soul eventually met Brian's. The two broken souls reconnected and endured happily forever after.

EAN 9782960194302

Dépôt légal : février 2017

D/2017/14.037/1